Hannah

Hannah

A novel

Nellie E. Robertson

iUniverse, Inc.
New York Lincoln Shanghai

Hannah
A novel

Copyright © 2007 by Nellie E. Robertson

All rights reserved. No part of this book may be used or reproduced by any means, graphic, electronic, or mechanical, including photocopying, recording, taping or by any information storage retrieval system without the written permission of the publisher except in the case of brief quotations embodied in critical articles and reviews.

iUniverse books may be ordered through booksellers or by contacting:

iUniverse
2021 Pine Lake Road, Suite 100
Lincoln, NE 68512
www.iuniverse.com
1-800-Authors (1-800-288-4677)

ISBN: 978-0-595-43062-8 (pbk)
ISBN: 978-0-595-68201-0 (cloth)
ISBN: 978-0-595-87404-0 (ebk)

Printed in the United States of America

Certain characters in this work are historical figures, and certain events portrayed did take place. However, this is a work of fiction. All of the other characters, names, and events as well as all places, incidents, organizations, and dialogue in this novel are either the products of the author's imagination or are used fictitiously.

Cover Photo

The picture on "Hannah's" cover is a photo of the Gold Bar Restaurant on Olympia's Main Street (now Capitol Way) just north of State Street. It was taken shortly before its demolition about 1911. The photo is used courtesy of the Washington State Historical Society.

Author's Note

The novels I have written are fictional stories surrounding historical facts. This book is no exception. As authors and reporters know, the writer is only as accurate as his sources. So it is with my work.

For the first time, I've abandoned Snohomish County in Washington State as my venue and found myself back at my birthplace in Thurston County. My research took me on a voyage of discovery about Olympia; facts I never knew growing up here, each and every one exciting. The things I've learned are fascinating and serve as a wonderful background for the story of "Hannah."

Appreciation goes to my son, Robert "Barney" Wagner for his financial support in publishing this novel; to my daughter, Billie Wayt, for her evaluation and contribution of ideas for it, and to my six great proof readers who keep me on my toes. They are listed in the bibliography.

Nellie E. Robertson
nelleva@msn.com

Foreword

You are hereby invited to a good read. Along with providing a good read, Nellie Robertson enriches us with interesting facts and information about the nascent years of Olympia, Washington Territory and Thurston County. We are not simply entertained. We learn something about the Bigelow residence, Priest's Point, the Gold Bar Restaurant and of other people, places and events.

The novel's characters are sharply sculpted giving us clear insight into their thoughts and motives as they go about building a life in the pioneer community. Qualities of integrity, cooperation, perseverance and loyalty illuminate each chapter. These, in counterpoint to hubris, self pity and ulterior motives make the characters come realistically alive.

Unabashedly, this is a romantic novel. Love and deeply intimate feelings move the principal characters forward as they build new lives for themselves and for the community which they have chosen.

Gift yourself.... read on!

Paul Moody
Senior Services for South Sound board member
Priest Point Park naturalist

Chapter One

The war was over and so was my life. My husband and my child were gone.

I had lived in Philadelphia working as a librarian when my world changed dramatically. I was not a beauty. I was tall for a woman, with a long face, prominent cheekbones and a smattering of freckles across my nose. My crowning feature was a head full of deep auburn hair. A handsome southerner with gracious manners and melodious voice stole my heart and took me to his Ruby Acres plantation in North Carolina as his wife.

As hard as I tried, I never changed into a southern belle and John Jewell's extended family did little to welcome this Yankee into their ranks. I wanted to clench my fists and scream at them that I was as good as they even though I had been born and raised in the north.

When the War Between the States started, John and I had been married five years and had a delightful little girl named Pearl who would be the epitome of southern womanhood, a state I never did attain. She resembled her father with blonde curls, slim stature, and a sunny disposition. She had my curiosity and intensity but without my aggressive nature.

John went to war in rebel gray and I protected our daughter as best I could. My heart tore into pieces, half with the north of my roots and half with my adopted south.

As I sat in my old wooden rocking chair on the slave cabin porch, the only structure left standing, contemplating the past, I read the letter in my hand for the fifth time sifting the nuances it contained and trying to read between the lines. It asked me to cross the continent to the Pacific Northwest to help my brother Andrew raise his young daughter after his wife's death.

A daughter, I thought. I'd lost mine to a wasting disease when there was nothing with which to treat her, not even decent food. Andrew and his girl were my only living relatives. We had lost our parents one by one before the war. Tears coursed down my cheeks as I recalled the fight I'd waged to keep my daughter alive. We nearly starved to death after Ruby Acres had been ravaged by men dressed in blue. I could still see parts of the burned ante-bellum home poking into the sky. I had come to love it in spite of being a Yankee.

A confederate soldier, ragged and unkempt, leaning on a makeshift crutch, had handed me a wrinkled letter several months before the end of the war. Written by John, it became his last words to me. He wanted me to leave the south and go where I would feel cherished and safe. He had written it from a hospital bed and his last words were, "If you receive this letter, I won't be coming home to you." I had read that letter so many times with tears splotching its surface that I could hardly read it any more. I questioned the man who had given it to me but he knew nothing. He said it had been passed from hand to hand on its trip to me.

Now I had a new letter to read and somebody really needed me. Could I leave this place where my most beloved family remained under southern soil? I vowed to never cry again. I had shed enough tears to water the whole plantation, what was left of it.

"Miz Hannah, honey, now don't you cry no matter what that old letter says," said the only darkie who had remained with me. With Lucy's unruly hair wrapped in a bandana and her short frame encased in a worn dress that dragged in the dirt, she comforted me in the best way she knew how. Her cherubic face had become as gaunt as mine. Her light-colored skin bespoke of a white father who no doubt ploughed the women in the slave quarters and didn't acknowledge his by-blows.

"You're right, Lucy, I shouldn't cry any more. I can't undo the past." I heaved a sigh and thought of my brother's letter. The question I asked myself was if there was any reason to stay here. Of course the answer I knew was negative. I had to do something positive instead of acting like a helpless ninny who cried at the drop of a memory. "I would do anything if only I could hear John's voice again," I mumbled to myself. I loved that wonderful baritone southern drawl.

"Lucy, I'm going to Richmond to see if I can find out precisely what happened to John. If I don't get any answers there, I'll go on to Washington. Surely they'll have records about the prisoner of war camps. When I come back here we'll get ready for the trip to the Northwest. My brother Andrew wants me to come help raise his daughter and I'll be glad to leave this nightmare. I'd like you to come with me." I looked at her, my only friend, companion and servant. She had been freed but had nowhere to go, either. "It's your decision, Lucy. Tell me when I get back. Now I'll send a letter to Andrew asking for the travel money." How demeaning to beg for money.

I walked to town in order to catch the coach for the Confederate capital in Richmond. Lucy and I had spruced up my black gown as best we could and it hid my mended petticoats. Since my shoes had worn through, I put heavy canvas patches inside them to cover the holes. I'd keep my feet decorously on the ground so no one could detect the deplorable condition of my footwear. I dug into my carefully hoarded cash to pay for my fare.

The trip of discovery yielded no information at all and taxed what little patience I had left. Harried officials sent me from one place to another. It seemed the South's records were in a shambles. I did find out that John had been in a prison hospital but where and what had happened to him remained a mystery.

From Richmond, I took the coach north to Washington. The Yankee records were in a little better shape. John was listed as a prisoner of war and in a prison hospital with unspecified injuries. "I see that they had an outbreak of typhoid fever in that hospital and many died," the keeper of the records said. "We have no list of those who succumbed. I'm sorry, ma'am. That's all I can tell you," he said wearily. "Leave your name and address with me and if anything turns up, I'll write to you."

I gave him my brother's address and explained my move. He nodded and turned away to the long line of others who searched for answers.

Back at Ruby Acres, I felt despair with so many unanswered questions. Would I ever find the answers? In frustration I decided I had to focus on the future and not the past. "Well, Lucy, have you decided to go with me?" I asked hoping for an affirmative answer. The idea of traveling all that distance alone became a daunting thought.

"Yes, Miz Hannah, I want to go, too. I ain't got nobody here no more. I jumped the broom with my Tom but he went off with Massa John. He never come back neither," she said with misty eyes.

I glanced at her and said, "Fine. I'm glad you decided to go with me. We have two choices. We can go by stagecoach clear across the country or we can sail around Cape Horn to San Francisco. I'm inclined to go by ship. We'd have living quarters whereas in a coach, we'd have to stop at way stations."

We looked at each other, pondered the alternatives and finally I asked, "Do you get seasick?"

"I don't know, Miz Hannah, I ain't never been on a boat afore."

"We'll find out. As soon as I get the bank draft from Andrew, I'll make arrangements to go around the Horn. We have a month to get ready. Since the bank foreclosed on Ruby Acres, we have literally no assets." I thought about all of the loss. Fortunately, I had saved some gowns that were pretty well worn by now but we'd mend and patch.

Both of us were adept with needles so the preparations began. I became excited about our coming adventure. I'd always keenly feel my losses but looking forward instead of backward gave me a reason to live.

With so little to carry, we lugged our bags to town and caught the coach for New York. That in itself was a long, weary trip but we had to board the ship in that northern seaport. Our journey to the future had begun in the year of our Lord 1866.

Chapter Two

Lucy and I stood on the dock in New York with our possessions around us waiting for the lighter that would take us to the *Lady Eagle*. "That's really a beautiful boat, isn't it, Lucy?" I said as I breathed in the salt tang in the air. It was so good to be away from all the desolation of Ruby Acres and its painful memories. My last visit to the family graveyard nearly undid me when I said a last farewell to Pearl, my darling little girl.

A man on the dock heard my remark and said, "That's a clipper ship, lady, not a boat." He puffed himself up with superior knowledge.

"How can you tell?" I asked with my usual curiosity.

"Because of the raked masts," he said. "The way the masts lean backwards, so to speak, and the heavy spars make it possible for the ship to carry more canvas so it's a very fast ship. The overhanging stern is typical of the clipper ship. She's sure a beauty, ain't she?"

"Yes, she certainly is. I can hardly wait to see her with her sails set," I answered, anxious to be on my way. I wondered how long it would take us to get to San Francisco.

As I watched the loading of the ship, I saw the crane lift a wheeled device and swing it into the hold. It seemed as tall as a man and about fifteen feet long but I couldn't for the life of me figure out what it was. I'd have plenty of time to find out, I thought. Just then, the lighter touched the dock. We boarded with the help of the man at the tiller and our water journey began.

As we boarded, Captain Newman greeted us. "The steward will conduct you to your cabin, Mrs. Jewel, and we have bunks in the forward hold for servants." He motioned to the steward.

"Captain, I expressly asked for a cabin with two bunks. Lucy will stay with me'" I said with determination.

"But servants would be more comfortable with their own," he remonstrated.

"Lucy is not a servant. She's free and she's my companion. She'll stay with me."

Again the captain tried to convince me to have Lucy stay with the servants.

"Captain, are you hard of hearing?"

"Why, no, I hear very well," he said obviously puzzled.

"Then hear this: Lucy will be with me in my cabin which has been paid for in full. Is that understood?"

He shrugged his shoulders and motioned for the steward to show us to our quarters. We settled ourselves, laying out what we'd need and storing the rest in our baggage.

Lucy proved to be a poor sailor. As soon as the *Lady Eagle* cleared the port of New York, nausea overcame her and for the next few days, I cared for her. I emptied the slops over the side, applied wet cloths to her forehead, and fed her any dry food I could garner from the galley.

When she seemed a bit better, I went up on deck to catch a few reviving breaths of sea air. I leaned on the rail watching the wake of the ship and looking up at the vast array of sails the ship carried. The man on the dock was right. She was a majestic sight.

I felt someone lean on the rail beside me. I backed away and looked up at him. I was a tall woman, gaunt of frame after my lack of adequate diet. My prominent cheekbones did not lend themselves to beauty. I knew I was plain with freckles dancing across my nose but I clothed myself in dignity. The wind tore wisps of my hair from the bun encased in a snood.

"Excuse me, ma'am, but the captain told me you're going to Olympia in Washington Territory." He topped me by several inches but seemed shy as if he hadn't had much opportunity to talk to women. A black hat tilted over his dark hair and his smokey blue eyes twinkled.

"I don't think the captain had the right to tell you of my destination, but yes, we're going to Olympia."

"Well, he probably told us because that's where we're headed, too," the lanky man said with his shy smile

"You and your wife?" I asked

"No, me and my partner. We came east to buy a fire engine for the town. We formed a hook and ladder company six years ago, the first in Washington Territory, and this is our first hand-pumper engine. It's a used engine but it will serve us very well."

"Was that the contraption I saw being loaded? The one with wheels and sort of tubing around and over the top?"

"Yes, ma'am. That's the Columbia engine. I'll give you a personal introduction if you'd like," he said. "It gets kind of boring aboard ship."

"Well, I don't have time right now. I just came out for a breath of air. My traveling companion is very seasick so I have to go take care of her. Maybe later?"

"Just let me know," he replied.

"By the way, what's your name?"

"Just call me Jake," he said, "and my buddy is Ernie."

"I'm Mrs. Jewell," I told him, "and my companion is Lucy." With that I went down the companionway. All sorts of questions came to mind about my new acquaintance.

Lucy seemed to get her sea legs and started doing things for herself. She refused to go to the dining room knowing that most of the passengers were white and might be offended by her presence. No matter how I remonstrated with her, she remained adamant. Had she been a slave, she would have obeyed. I brought her food from the galley and then went up on deck to watch the waves and the sails.

"You are a real sailor, Mrs. Jewell," said Captain Newman as he strode up to me and leaned on the rail. He was a bit shorter than I with mutton chop whiskers lining his chin. His blue eyes matched the ocean he sailed.

"I guess so, although I've never been on a ship before. This is such a glorious sight, the blue water, the white sails filled with the wind and the cotton clouds," I said with enthusiasm.

"I'm afraid the clipper ship is a dying breed. With steam vessels coming off the ways daily, it won't be long until sails are replaced completely except for some freighting and pleasure uses." I enjoyed listening to his Yankee twang that reminded me of home.

"That will be a sad time, to lose all this beauty and style for a noisy, smelly steam vessel," I sighed.

"When the sails go, so do I," said the captain, natty in his double-breasted blue coat with brass buttons. "I've earned my retirement but, still, it will be hard to leave the sea." He smoothed his gray whiskers with an index finger.

"You're a young man, captain. Surely you've got years yet to retirement?"

"I've been sailing for nearly 30 years, Mrs. Jewell, and steam isn't in my future. No doubt I'll live near the water and enjoy watching the tides and clouds but I'll be reliving the past." He pulled out his big gold watch attached to his pocket by a hefty gold chain, and flipped open the case. "I have to get back to work now, Mrs. Jewell. It's good to talk to someone who understands. See you at supper. You're invited to sit at my table."

As I entered the dining saloon, I took note of the faded red carpet that bespoke of a more luxurious past and the polished brass fittings that shone against the dark paneling.

Supper at the captain's table was a real trial for me. I cannot abide bigotry and it sat at our table in the form of the heavy lady whose distaste for most everyone was printed on her sagging face.

"And where are you headed, Mrs. Jewell?" she asked with a sniff after we were introduced.

"I'm going to Washington Territory to care for my brother's little girl. His wife died and he's at his wits end." I revealed more than I should have but she irritated me so much.

"My, that's quite an undertaking," she replied. Drawing up her corseted self as best she could, she said, "I'm joining my husband in San Francisco. He's in banking and very important in the town."

I let her remarks slide over me and glanced around the dining saloon to take note of my few fellow travelers who sat at the other tables. Over in the corner I saw Jake and a dumpy little fellow who must be Ernie, just the opposite of Jake's tall frame. I saw that Jake watched me and the look in his smoky blue eyes gave me a jolt.

When I returned to the cabin after supper in the saloon, Lucy had set it to rights and now occupied one of the two squat chairs. A small stand filled the space between them. I had an instantaneous thought.

"Lucy, I'm going to teach you to read. Reading is the gateway to knowledge, they say. I have a few primers in my case so I can teach Abigail to read. I'll practice on you."

"Oh, no, Miz Hannah, I ain't supposed to have any learnin'" Lucy replied.

"This is not the south, Lucy, and you're a free woman. Learning to read will help you in our new home. It can lead to any number of wonderful things."

"If you say it's fine, I'll do it but I hope it don't get me into no trouble."

"I assure you it won't. Another thing I've decided is we'll go up on deck every morning before we have our lessons. You need to see this beautiful ship and smell the fresh salt air."

Lucy started to argue, then threw up her hands, "If you say so, Miz Hannah."

No doubt my determination showed on my face and she had succumbed to my dictates many times. She knew I would persevere.

As we readied ourselves for bed, I fingered the cameo locket that had belonged to my mother. It was the only memento I had from her, and inside a curl of golden hair was all that remained of my baby.

The next morning, as Lucy and I opened our cabin door, the hefty woman from the captain's table dressed in black glared at my companion, sniffed, and continued on her way down the companionway. Her girth nearly reached both sides of the passage. How righteous she thought herself, no doubt. I thought it too bad that her size didn't match her narrow mind. I felt like giving her a handkerchief for her sniff.

Lucy gazed with wonder at the white sails and the wake the ship made. She breathed deeply and threw her arms wide. "Oh, Miz Hannah, I didn't dream this would be so fine."

"It is fine, Lucy, and we'll enjoy it every morning."

We ambled around the deck avoiding any of the sailors who worked to keep the ship in trim. The captain had told me the crew numbered 35. I wondered if we'd meet Jake.

Chapter Three

While Lucy took a nap, I went up on deck. It seemed I couldn't stay away from the awesome flight of the *Lady Eagle*. The vista changed hourly yet stayed the same. The further south we went, the warmer and muggier the climate became. It seemed strange that the breeze that bellied the sails did little to relieve the heavy heat.

As I gazed off into the distance, Jake came to lean on the rail beside me. "And how does it go with Jake?" I asked, pleased at his appearance.

"Just fine, Mrs. Jewell. I'm a good sailor but Ernie's had a tough time. Puget Sound sailing is nothing like this." He stretched his lanky frame to its full height. "I'll be glad to get past the equator and into the southern latitudes. It's fall down there and it should be cooler."

"I've read so much about Cape Horn. I wonder how turbulent the weather will be going around it," I said.

"You'll have to ask the captain about that," Jake replied in his laconic manner that I enjoyed. "Care to take a turn around the deck?"

"I would if I knew your last name."

"It's Buss with a double 's.' Some of the jokers call me Blunderbuss if they're out of my reach," he laughed, deep in his chest.

We strolled along the rail avoiding the sailors whose work was never done. I tripped over a cable and Jake caught my arm. It sent an electric shock through my whole body. I'd never felt such a flood of feeling in my life.

"I think we should call you 'blunderbuss', Mrs. Jewell," he laughed.

"You may be right, Jake, and it's about time you called me Hannah." I smiled and wondered why my face didn't crack. It wasn't used to smiling.

"Hannah it is. Will Mr. Jewell join you in Olympia?"

His question hung in the air for a minute or two. "There is no longer a Mr. Jewell. He did not survive the late unpleasantness between the states."

"Oh, Hannah, I'm so sorry. I'd like to hear the rest of that story."

"Maybe later, Jake. Right now I must go down to check on Lucy. Thanks for the companionship. It's been so long since I've enjoyed the company of contemporaries."

After the next morning's lessons, we heard a knock on the door. I opened it cautiously to find Jake at the door, black hat in hand.

"Would you like to see our fire engine now, Hannah?" he asked as he shyly ducked his head.

"Yes, I would, Jake, I'll meet you on deck in a few minutes."

After looking into the shiny piece of metal that served as a mirror, I realized I couldn't do much to improve my plain appearance and put my disappointment aside. I am me, I thought, and I accept that, almost, although recognizing one's shortcomings proved difficult.

On deck, Jake took my arm again with the same shock to my senses, and led me down the companionway into the bowels of the ship. Lanterns hung here and there to light our way but the gloom pervaded. We arrived at the contraption and I got a lecture on its use and value. The center was flanked by two arms connected to the drum and men would move them up and down to pump water on the fire. Horses would draw it to its destination.

Overwhelmed with the process and the device itself, I murmured, "What an extraordinary machine. Have you seen it in action?"

"Oh, yes, Ernie and I were given instructions to try it out first before we plunked down the money. The whole crew will be so proud of it." His slightly lopsided smile nearly undid me. This couldn't be happening to plain Hannah. It must be my imagination.

As we made our way up the companionway, he steadied my steps. The fresh salt air erased the stuffiness of the hold even though the heat was still oppressive.

"Do you have to eat at the captain's table?" he asked stubbing his toe into the planking.

"No, I guess not, and I really have nothing in common with some of those stuffed shirts although I do enjoy the captain's company."

He glowered a bit then asked, "Ernie and me would like you to have supper with us tonight if you can arrange it." The hopeful look on his face reminded me of my brother when he was very young.

"Thank you. I'd like to dine with you," I said and found that I really wanted to share the time with Jake.

I searched for the captain and finally found him berating a couple of his crew. I stood aside until he finished then told him I'd have supper with Jake and Ernie.

"I'm disappointed, Mrs. Jewell, you're the one bright spot at the table. Some of those honored to sit there bore me but don't tell them. I'm doing my job as captain."

"How long will it take us to get to San Francisco?" I asked, posing a question I had wanted to ask numerous times.

"Well, there's no easy answer. The *Flying Cloud* set the record at 89 days but we won't come close to that. I'd say four months from New York give or take a week or two depending on the weather around the Horn."

"I've been concerned about that. Is this a good time of year to tackle the Horn?" I asked concerned that Lucy would get seasick again.

"You can never predict the troublesome waters there," Captain Newman responded. "Cape Horn has been loved and hated for over three hundred years. It lays where the continental shelf rises from the deep Pacific bed off the southern coast of Argentina and where the strong forces of the winds that blow around Antarctica often create gales with waves that are frequently more than 65 feet high." He paused as if to collect the rest of his thoughts.

"Seamen say there are an average of 200 days of gale and 130 days of cloudy sky. As for the rest of the year, the wind is strong and the sea is rough. It's really a crap shoot, pardon the language, but we have no alternative if we want to take this route to the west coast." A seaman knuckled his forehead and the captain apologized as he turned to his duty.

As the afternoon progressed, I lay down to rest before joining Jake for supper. The anticipation felt strange to me. I couldn't understand this attraction. I had experienced the love of my life yet I had never felt such electricity when I was in John's arms. I got little rest with these thoughts going through my mind.

I carefully chose my best gown, twisted my hair into a bun at the back of my head and no matter how I tried to smooth the curly tendrils, they escaped from the twist. I looked into the makeshift mirror, gave a last pat to my hair, and told Lucy I'd bring her supper in a little while. I left our cabin with anticipation.

Chapter Four

As I entered the dining saloon, I spotted Jake at his usual table without his companion. Somehow, I felt relieved. My few glimpses of dumpy Ernie made me realize he'd spoil the rapport I felt with Jake.

The lanky guy stood and ushered me into the bench across from where he sat. The moment seemed awkward at first as if we had never met before. This was not a casual meeting at the rail but in a dining saloon with others sitting at various tables.

"I'm glad you decided to eat with me tonight," Jake began, clearing his throat.

"So am I, Jake. I really didn't enjoy the snobs at the captain's table, and I might add Captain Newman agreed with me." I loosened my wrap, patted my hair, and read the brief menu.

After we chose our entrees, we looked at each other and it seemed neither of us could tear our eyes away.

I cleared my throat, "With your huge black hat and the drawl you try to conceal, I think you were a cowhand," I said with a smile. "Tell me all about Jake."

"I will if you reply in kind," he said emphasizing the drawl. "Deal?"

"It looks like we've made a pact, Jake. Begin."

"You're right on two counts. I was a cowhand and I do have a Texas drawl. I punched cattle on my daddy's spread in west Texas. When the War Between the States kicked off, I didn't want to be any part of it so I lit out for places unknown." He ducked his head shyly.

"Keep on, young man; I want to hear it all." While he talked I ate although I was much more interested in his tale than the food on my plate.

"Well, I hitched a ride with a wagon train going west and worked my way helping with the livestock. We hit the Willamette Valley in Oregon Territory but it was too crowded there so I went with another group headed up the Cowlitz Trail and ended up at Olympia." He munched for a while and I got a question in before he swallowed.

"How did Olympia perceive the war?"

"They were mostly pro-union but again bigotry took a toehold. The people don't want colored folks around."

"You know I have a colored companion. How will she be treated, do you think?"

"George Washington Bush is a mulatto and helped settle New Market, now Tumwater, because of the falls of the Deschutes River. He helped those people so much that he's accepted and the prairie's named for him. The government tried to take his land away from him since men of color weren't allowed to own land in the United States but his fellow pioneers rallied around, hit the national capitol, and he and his descendents have the land forever. How they'll treat your companion, I have no idea. I guess maybe it depends on how she acts." His smoky blue eyes reached clear into my soul. "They'll accept you, though, without reservation. Women are scarce in Washington Territory."

"You mean a plain woman like me might be in demand?"

"You're not plain, Hannah You're a beautiful woman."

"You know I'm not comely, Mr. Buss," I said with alacrity.

"To me, you are, Hannah," he replied.

I chose to lighten the exchange. "Is there a Mrs. Buss, Mr. Blunderbuss?"

"Nope, not yet, but that could change," he said with a direct look at me. "Now, it's your turn. Tell me all about Hannah."

"There's really not a whole lot to tell and most of it painful. I served as a librarian in Philadelphia when this charming southern gentleman appeared and swept me off my feet. We married and he took me back to his Ruby Acres where all of the belles disapproved of this Yankee. I tried hard to fit in and become a southern belle too, for John's sake, but can you imagine me frittering away my time in needlepoint and idle chatter?"

"Not really, but then I don't know you that well."

"We had a delightful little girl named Pearl. The war started five years after we married. John joined the rebel army and I tried to keep things going on the plantation. Several months before the end of hostilities, I got a note from him saying that if I got the letter, he wouldn't be coming back. My daughter literally died in my arms without medicine and decent food to sustain her." Tears streamed down my face.

"Let's get out of here," Jake said, and ushered me out the door to the ship's rail.

"I vowed never to cry again. I'm sorry," I hiccupped.

He put his arm around my shoulders and I leaned into his strong frame. Never had anyone consoled me in such a manner about my losses. How wonderful it was to relax into his strength.

"Okay, Hannah, tell the rest of the story and then we'll go from there. What happened to all of the 'belles' you talked about?"

"The ones I had truck with were useless. I tried to keep things together so there'd be something left when John returned. We received word that the Yankees would be in the area within a few days. All of a sudden, the 'belles' lit out with everything they could carry. The boys in blue came, devastated the plantation then burned the plantation's main house and all of the outbuildings except one. Lucy and I ended up in the only slave cabin left standing. Why it wasn't burned too, I'll never understand."

I wiped away my tears, and continued, "My brother wrote to me from Olympia and asked if I would come and help raise his daughter. His wife had died and he had a hard time caring for her and trying to prove up on his homestead. That's it. That's why I'm on this vessel, standing at the rail with a tall Texan."

"If men cried, I'd cry with you, but of course we Texans are very manly," he said in his Texas drawl. "You've experienced some terrible events but now they're over and you can look forward to a wonderful life in beautiful Washington Territory."

"I'd like to hear more about my destination but I have to go get Lucy's supper. She's probably starving. Since she had gotten over her mal-de-mer she's ravenous."

Jake kept his arm loosely around my shoulders and guided me toward the dining saloon.

Chapter Five

The change of weather produced a welcome chill after the humid heat of the past two weeks. The sails billowed out snapping in the freshening wind. I unbound my bun and let the wind rake through my hair. I exulted in the feeling of freedom. I was alone on deck and thought about Jake and the attraction he held for me. It was idiotic, of course, it could lead nowhere, but dreaming of things that could not be was a way for me to escape the past.

I headed toward our cabin and another reading lesson for Lucy. She did so well I thought she had a natural bent for the written word. As we settled next to each other on one of the bunks, I put my wire-rimmed glasses on my nose and became engrossed in the teaching at hand.

A tentative rap on the door startled both Lucy and me. She quickly moved to the other bunk and I went to the door. Jake stood there, black hat in hand and seemed a little taken aback.

"Is something wrong, Jake?" I asked.

"Well, no. I guess I've never seen you with glasses on before. It shook me some."

"I wear them only for reading and needlework." I whipped them off and put them into a pocket. "Was there something you wanted, Jake?"

"Yes, ma'am, I wanted to make sure you'd be at our table for supper tonight." He dug his toe into the floor again. I'd noticed this was his way of expressing his shyness.

"Yes, certainly, if I wouldn't be intruding."

"No, Hannah, you'd light up our table." He favored me with his crooked smile.

"Come in, Jake, I want you to meet my traveling companion." I pulled him in by his arm and faced him toward the young woman practically crouched on the cot. "This is Lucy, my closest friend."

"I'm right glad to meet you, Lucy. I hear you're learning to read."

The panic on Lucy's face was readily apparent as she cowered on the bunk.

"It's fine, Lucy, you have nothing to fear from Jake. He's our friend." She nodded but said not one word.

"I'll see you at supper, Hannah, and Lucy's invited if she'd like to come."

Again voiceless, Lucy just shook her head in denial.

"Maybe some other time, Jake. I'll see you in the saloon."

To my disappointment I saw that Ernie sat at the supper table, too. He seemed to bounce around with excess energy like a big rubber ball. We gave our orders to the steward and settled in to wait for our food.

"So, gentlemen, tell me about Olympia's background. My brother told me nothing about it, past or present." I put on my most rapt expression and waited.

Ernie was the first to respond in his staccato way of speaking. "Well, I love history even though Olympia really isn't that old. It was founded in 1850 and incorporated in 1859. Edmund Sylvester and Levi Smith jointly claimed the land that is now Olympia. They called it Smithfield at first. Smith died in 1848 so it all went to Sylvester." He paused to take a breath. "Smith had a tragic accident. He was in his canoe on the way to Tumwater when he had an epileptic fit, fell out of the canoe and drowned." He shook his head in mock disbelief.

"How did the name change to Olympia" I asked, "and is it named for Olympia in Greece?"

Again, Ernie jumped into the breach, "Well, there's two ways of thinking on that. Some believe Sylvester changed the name, others say Colonel Eby did. In any case, it was named for the Olympic Mountains on the peninsula." He wiped the spittle from his lips with his napkin.

In the pause, I asked, "Are the mountains very high?"

This time, Jake answered before Ernie could draw a breath. "They are higher than anything you've ever seen, I bet. And the Cascade Mountains cut the territory in half so you're surrounded by snow-capped mountains the year round with seas of big, very big, trees."

"My, you wax poetic, Jake, I didn't know you had it in you," I said archly.

He just smiled and looked at me with those smoky blue eyes of his that held a wealth of feeling.

Ernie broke the spell. "Washington Territory was created by breaking it off from the Oregon Territory at the Columbia River. When old Isaac Stevens, the first governor, arrived, he named the town the capitol of the territory. The story went around that when he came to town, he arrived early and scruffy-looking so nobody recognized him as the new governor. The first territorial legislature was held in the Gold Bar Restaurant right there on Main Street."

The next question hovered on my lips. I wanted Jake to answer so I waited until Ernie had a mouthful of mashed potatoes and asked, "How are you going to get your fire engine to Olympia from San Francisco?"

Jake read my ploy and answered, "We're taking a brig up the coast and into Puget Sound. The arrangements were made before we ever traveled cross country to New York." He sat back, looked at me as if evaluating me and posed a question of his own. "How are you getting there?"

"I thought I'd book passage on some vessel. I hate the thought of trying to go overland. I considered taking a stagecoach across the continent but thought it would be a very tedious journey so I took to the water."

"They ought to have room on the brig for two more passengers. As soon as we get in, I'll check on it for you, that is if you still want the Olympia Fire Department as your guide. You'll be sailing on an historic ship, too. The *Orbit* was the first sea-going ship on Puget Sound owned by Olympians and is still going strong even though she's up in years."

"That relieves my mind considerably," I breathed. It had bothered me for some time how we'd complete our journey. "I'm anxious to get to my destination and see my brother. You don't know him by any chance, do you?"

"What's his name?" Ernie asked, now that his food had gone down his throat.

"His name is Andrew Delaney. He's tall and lanky with bright red hair. We used to resemble one another but I haven't seen him for years so he might have changed. His daughter, Abigail, is about six if I remember correctly."

The two men looked blankly at one another. "I guess that answers my question," I said. "He's proving up on a homestead and does some logging, too, I think."

"Ernie here is a logger and I have a draying business. As a west Texan, I have an affinity with horses. We get along just fine."

I turned to Ernie and asked, "Is there a lot of logging going on in the area?"

"You bet," he sputtered. "That's the main industry these days. There's just no end to the trees and they're bigger than any forests on the east coast that I saw."

"How'd you get to Washington Territory?" I asked looking at the rotund little man. He didn't fit my vision of a brawny logger.

"About the same way Jake did, overland to the Willamette Valley then north on the Cowlitz trail. Too bad we couldn't take the engine back the same way. Then I wouldn't have been seasick. Oh, well, live and learn."

Jake asked me to take a stroll with him on deck but I excused myself and went to the galley to get Lucy's supper. I thought being near him alone could lead me in a direction I shouldn't travel.

The further south we sailed, the rougher the passage. The captain told me we approached Cape Horn and to be prepared for whatever the Fates might throw our way. As I lay in my bunk that night, thoughts of my two supper companions lingered in my head. I tried to bring back the feeling I'd had for John but other thoughts kept getting in the way. I drifted off to sleep only to wake to the erratic movement of the ship.

Chapter Six

I clung to my berth with both of my hands to keep from pitching to the deck of the cabin. Lucy did the same. Both of us threw up at the same time. It registered in my mind that we must be going around the Horn. The *Lady Eagle* lost her composure as she ploughed, pitched, rolled, dipped and soared through the maelstrom that comprised the ocean at the southern tip of Argentina. The ship staggered uphill, tottered on the crests of the waves then plunged to the depth of troughs.

In our small cabin, we ministered to each other as well as we could and had no yearning for food. Our stomachs couldn't tolerate the thought of sustenance. We just prayed for it to be over.

A knock came on our cabin door. I called with little volume to go away. The knock came again and I tottered to the door ready to spend what little energy I had to make the caller go away and leave us alone.

Jake stood in the doorway, smiling shyly. "I seem to be the only one who's not seasick. I thought you and Lucy might need some help."

"We're helping each other and there's little you can do, Jake. Thanks anyway." I pushed back my unkempt mop of hair and started to close the door.

"I'm going to empty your slops whether you like it or not and I've brought some fresh, cold cloths for your foreheads. I've got some water here and some dry toast. Now, quit protesting, and get back to your bunk," he said forcefully.

As weak as I was, I did as he said. Relief filled me. Here was someone to take charge and succor these two very seasick women. I had always been the one in command and it felt good to let go and have Jake take over. I slipped into a doze.

It seemed like weeks passed before the turmoil of going around Cape Horn finally eased. I could empathize with Lucy whose second bout of seasickness left her lethargic and gaunt with the lack of food. She began to eat again and I got my sea legs under me once more as we sailed up the western coast of South America and California to San Francisco. It didn't take long for me to become my old self again with Jake's help.

The city of San Francisco splayed out from the main bulk of the continent with streets leading into its interior from different parts of the coastline. Tall buildings punctured the sky and shorter structures surrounded them. From what we could discern from the *Lady Eagle*, it was a beehive of human activity, each individual bee intent on its own pursuits.

The idle ships surrounded three sides of the land mass and ranged from the tallest ships with multiple masts to tiny, one-masted coasters. A few steam vessels belched smoke into the cloudless sky.

As Lucy and I awaited the passenger lighter to take us ashore, Jake and Ernie came alongside us and watched all of the activity. I turned to Jake and asked, "Do you see the *Orbit*?"

"I really can't be sure. I know it is a two-masted square-rigger and the fire engine will have to be lashed to the deck. It won't fit in the hold. Coast Transportation is the name of the booking office." We both scanned the sea around us and found several ships with two masts but couldn't discern what might be our next vessel.

"After we supervise the transfer of our engine, I'll find you at Coast Transportation. Will you wait there for me?" Jake asked.

I nodded and we said, "'till later" with our eyes.

When our feet finally touched dry land, Lucy and I both heaved sighs of relief although we still swayed with remembered ship motion. We needed to cultivate our land legs. So much energy swirled around us we felt caught in a maelstrom of activity.

We finally hailed a hansom to haul us and our luggage to the Coast Transportation office. The driver helped us unload all of our trappings and we entered the office. I walked to the desk and told the clerk we needed two tickets to Olympia on the *Orbit*.

He frowned. "Just a minute, ma'am, and I'll help you."

Lucy moved her lips as she read some of the posters on the wall. My chest burst with pride at what we had accomplished together during our voyage. Her language had changed a great deal, too. Little trace was left of the submissive slave words.

The clerk waved me over to the counter. "I'm sorry ma'am but that vessel is full. We have no more cabin space for passengers. You'll have to wait until the next voyage going there."

"Oh, but we can't stay here. We must get to Olympia," I said with a sinking heart. To come this far and then have to wait was intolerable.

Just then a tall woman, dressed in the latest fashion with a bonnet perched on her gray curls moved out of the shadows and said in her whiskey voice, "Honey, you and your maid can bunk in my cabin. It's large enough for three of us." She took a dainty handkerchief out of her cuff and wiped her lips. The lip paint came off on the kerchief.

I looked at Lucy then back to the woman knowing that I had to accept her offer. "Thank you very much, ma'am. I'm sorry; I didn't hear your name."

"I'm Zona and I've been hired to run the Gold Bar Restaurant and Saloon in Olympia." Her half smile gave her a sardonic look. I felt that nothing could faze this lady with a wealth of experience in her steady gaze.

"Does Zona have a last name?" I asked answering her smile.

"Zona's been good enough for me for a lot of years, honey. I've managed a number of saloons, the last one in Kansas City, so I've been around and everyone knows Zona with no last name." She certainly piqued my interest and I thought I'd slake that curiosity on our trip up the coast.

"I think I have to make one thing clear," I began. "Lucy is not my maid, she's my companion. We're the only two left of a grand plantation in North Carolina." It seemed I always had to explain this relationship if Lucy were to have a chance at a new life in Olympia.

"Honey, I understand completely. I'd like to have someone like her to help me at the Gold Bar. Maybe I can lure her away from you."

"That's entirely up to her," I said casting a glance at Lucy whose head was bowed.

"She knows how to read? I saw she was reading the posters." At those words, Lucy cowered behind me.

I threw up my head and said defiantly, "Yes, she does. I taught her on our voyage. She's a natural learner. She's not a slave so she can read if she wants to."

"Hey, babe, don't get your tail in a knot. It's fine by me. The more learning the better, I say." She patted my shoulder and my defiance left me.

"Do you know when we sail?" I asked wondering if we'd have to find lodging and how difficult that would be.

"Well, this young man here told me that as soon as the *Orbit* was loaded, we'd be off. He was waiting for the fire engine, he said. Does that make sense to you?"

"Oh, yes, the Columbia was on the *Lady Eagle* with us and the two firemen who sailed with it, Jake Buss and Ernie Ellis."

"Not Jake, the rake," she laughed. "I've heard about him and the ladies. He must be a charmer all right."

The wind went out of my sails, so to speak. I had never felt jealousy before but this must be it. So Jake of the smoky blue eyes and the electric touch was a lady's man and I had fallen for his act. I thought it time for a reality check on my emotions.

Chapter Seven

Zona agreed to watch for Jake while Lucy and I walked around the bustling town. It had been sixteen years since the Forty-niners had swamped these shores after the discovery of gold in California but the people we encountered were still intent on important business as they hurried along. A goodly number of Orientals filtered in among the whites, blacks, Indians and those of Spanish descent readily recognizable because of their beautiful tawny skin.

Spires and onion-shaped domes reared into the sky from churches and the buildings appeared solidly built except for along the vast shoreline. September sunshine warmed us as we strolled looking into shop windows and listening to street-corner orators. The atmosphere seemed so different from the east coast, a refreshing change. I wondered if Olympia would be the same.

We angled back to the transportation office hoping it would be time to board the *Orbit*. I didn't relish another voyage but I thought it better than trying to go overland. Zona still stood ramrod straight and said, "Jake, the rake, hasn't shown yet but he should be here soon, according to the clerk," nodding toward the guy behind the counter.

"Will the ship leave today or do we need to find lodgings?" I asked, hoping for the former.

With another nod at the clerk, Zona said, "We should be sailing today. I certainly hope so. I'm anxious to begin my new job. It will be a challenge. I've never managed a restaurant before but it can't be too different from running a saloon.

People are people." She looked around impatiently, "I'm not good at waiting." Again she wiped her lips with the lace handkerchief she tucked in her sleeve. She straightened her bonnet on the graying hair and smoothed her gown.

I looked out the window and saw Jake striding up the walk. He turned into the office and came directly to me. "Did you get your tickets?" he asked.

I pulled away from his grasp and replied, "Yes, I did. There were no more cabins so Zona, here, invited us to share her quarters. She's the new manager of the Gold Bar Restaurant in Olympia."

He turned to her and said, "I've spent some time in that establishment, Zona. I'm glad to meet you." His smile was wide and welcoming.

"Glad to meet you, too, Jake. I've heard about you," she said with a knowing smile as she scanned him from head to toe. "I can see what I heard could be true."

"I guess I don't want to hear what the gossips told you. I know you'll be a welcome addition to the Gold Bar Restaurant. It's where the first territorial legislature was held. Did you know that?"

"So I've been told. It's nice to join a little bit of history," Zona said with a smile. Jake returned her smile.

"Well, let's get this show on the road. The ship is loading now and I have a lighter waiting for us. The fire engine is lashed amidships. It looks awkward but it wouldn't fit in the hold." He reached for my shoulder and I ducked away. I didn't need any more of his smoldering eyes and electric touches. I would not be one of many.

His puzzled look created a frown on his forehead and I turned from him. Lucy and I gathered our baggage and a carriage appeared at Jake's whistle. The driver helped with Zona's trunk and her suitcases. It took some time threading through all of the traffic on busy San Francisco streets but we finally arrived at the shore.

When Jake tried to take my arm to help me board the lighter I jerked away and said with determination, "I can do it by myself, thank you."

We three women were shown to our cabin and indeed it was big enough for us. Zona had a pallet brought in for Lucy. It didn't take long for Lucy and me to settle in but with Zona's entire luggage, it took her considerable time. Lucy pitched in to help her and I couldn't resist going up on deck to watch our departure.

I loved the way the canvas sails snapped when sailors cinched them into place. As they bellied out I thought of a cartoon I had seen. It showed a cloud-like figure with lips pursed, cheeks filled with air, blowing with great force to fill the sails of an imaginary ship. White wisps of cotton lazed across the brilliant blue sky.

Jake put his elbows on the rail next to mine without touching me. "What's wrong, Hannah?" he asked with another puzzled look at me.

"I don't know what you're talking about, Jake, the rake," I said with some asperity.

"You're suddenly giving me the cold shoulder and you know it. Something's happened since we left the *Lady Eagle* and I want to know what it is." He put his hand on my arm and I pulled away.

"It's really nothing, Jake, except that I understand that you're quite a ladies' man and I really don't want to be one of the herd that dotes on you." I drew myself up, pushed back the stray locks of hair the wind had loosened from my bun and looked away from him.

"I don't know what you were told, Hannah, but how can you condemn me without a hearing. I have women friends just as I have men friends. It's normal. None of the women are more than acquaintances. In a small town like Olympia people become friends pretty easily and that's all they are to me, just friends." His earnest voice, almost pleading, caught me by surprise and I looked at him.

"I presumed too much about our relationship, Jake. Being such a plain woman, I haven't had much male attention so I read too much into your interest in me. I'm sorry. I guess I'm just a silly ninny." I turned back to watch the prow cut the quiet Pacific Ocean.

Jake put his hand under my chin and turned my face to him. "You're not plain and you're not a ninny. You're a special woman, Hannah."

I looked at him and wondered if he really thought that or if it were just one of his ploys in attracting women.

"I'm unattached, Hannah, and so are you. We are free to pursue any relationship we want," he said earnestly.

"You may be unattached, Jake, but I'm attached to a memory." I turned away.

Sailing up the Pacific Coast was a delight for a few days then the weather took a turn for the worse. Clouds gathered, wind blew and the waves tossed the ship around. Fortunately, the only one to succumb to mal-de-mer was Lucy. Zona took it all in her stride, a trait I would find supportive and comforting in my times of need.

Again, Jake joined me at the rail as I held my face up to the rain. I clutched the rail to keep the wind from blowing me away. "You look worried, Mr. Blunderbuss,"

"The captain's going to go further out to sea to get away from the turbulence off the mouth of the Columbia River. He said if he can't get to calmer water, we might have to jettison the fire engine and that doesn't bear thinking about. The guys would never forgive us." I saw a different Jake Buss from all the others I had seen. His concern manifested itself in his face and in his posture. He thought of nothing else but the horrible possibility of losing his charge.

The prow of the *Orbit* now pointed to the west, out of the battle the river and sea waged for supremacy. The ship shuddered on the new tack but she responded gallantly. The captain had told me that a brig could turn end to end under the guidance of a good skipper and he must be a good one because we made a quarter turn and the seas seemed to quiet a little although we were not in smooth water.

Jake continued to contemplate the machine lashed between the two hefty masts and I watched from the shelter of the companionway, holding the sides to keep from being blown away. What a disaster if the fire engine had to be thrown overboard after all the time, effort, and money that had gone into its journey. I could just imagine the firemen waiting at the Olympia dock. I was not yet a part of that community but I would feel its loss as well, like I already had a proprietary interest.

Jake and Ernie stood on each side of the engine glowering at the crewmen, a couple of whom had axes in case they needed to cut the hawsers that bound the engine between the masts. As the sea leveled out a bit, the sailors relaxed their determined stands and the two firemen flexed their shoulders and eased from their confrontational attitudes.

Chapter Eight

As we headed north again, the rain continued but the wind abated. It wasn't exactly smooth sailing but more tolerable. Since dining arrangements aboard the *Orbit* were less than satisfactory, we three women took turns going to the galley to get our meals. The food was hearty if not tasty. Lucy had survived again and up the coast we went.

I had asked the captain about this continuing rain. He'd told me to get used to it if I intended to live in Washington Territory. It enveloped the *Orbit* and I could no longer see the mast tops. The sails seemed to disappear into the ominous clouds.

When I returned to our cabin, Lucy and Zona talked to each other with animation. I had never seen Lucy come out of her shell like this.

"Glad you're here, honey," Zona said as she rose from her bunk. I realized that she was one of the few women I could look at eye to eye since we were the same height. "I want to hire this girl from you. She's just what I need at the Gold Bar. Everyone else will be strangers and I know Lucy. She'd be a godsend to me. Now before you answer, I assure you she'll be well cared for and protected. No one will hurt her and put her down." She ran out of breath and stopped.

"First of all, Lucy is free and can make her own decisions. No, you can't hire her from me because I don't employ her. It might be best since I don't know how much room my brother has in his cabin." I stopped a moment then continued, "I trust you, Zona, and if Lucy decides to work for you, I'll be content that she's doing what she wants to do." With that there were satisfied smiles all around and I knew Lucy's answer without her voicing it.

Jake and I leaned on the rail and watched the sea birds swooping around the ship. We had come to a tacit agreement that allowed for companionship but I still kept my emotional distance.

"We must be fairly close to land with the seagulls wheeling around us," I said.

"Although you can't see it, land is on our starboard side. If the sky were clear, we could see the Olympic Mountains. They're always snow-covered, really majestic." He straightened and continued, "We should be entering the Strait of Juan de Fuca soon. I hope it clears enough for you to see Canada on our left and Washington Territory on our right."

The mist continued to shroud the ship but I caught a glimmer of the two land masses Jake had mentioned when we began to sail eastward through the strait. Our long voyage would end very soon and I wondered what awaited me in Olympia.

The weather cleared somewhat as we began our voyage down Puget Sound and my mouth hung open in awe when I saw the beautiful mountain that reared into the sky surrounded by oceans of evergreen trees.

"Close your mouth, Hannah. That's Mount Rainier, part of the Cascade Mountain range. The Indians call it Mount Tahoma. Beautiful, isn't it?" Jake asked.

"Oh, yes, I've never seen anything like it," I replied. It had such raw grandeur.

The sun flirted with the rain clouds as the *Orbit* split the waters of the Sound like the gallant ship she was. The captain had told me the inland waterway had about 1,200 miles of shoreline with inlets, bays and harbors. He said the trip from the beginning of Puget Sound to Olympia covered about 95 miles as the crow flies.

Dusk fell as we anchored west of Seattle. Several passengers and their luggage were loaded into the small dinghy for the short trip to the little port town. As the skipper strolled up, I asked, "Will we continue on to Olympia tonight?"

"No, we're a little ahead of schedule so we'll anchor here and leave at dawn for the final leg of our journey." His long, narrow face appeared stern but I knew he had a lot on his mind. I had come to respect the knowledge and commitment of the two captains with whom I had sailed.

As the daylight touched our cabin window, I had to hurry up on deck to see this settlement. Maybe I could get a feel of the town I'd call home. I noticed the captain looking at the shoreline with his telescope.

"Here, Mrs. Jewell," he said handing the 'scope to me. "Focus on that big building on the hill with the dome. See it?"

"Oh, yes, it seems so much more modern than those buildings along the shore."

"That's the Territorial University of Washington."

"There's a university in the territory?" Without waiting for his answer I continued. "Is this place bigger than Olympia?"

"Not now. Seattle, named after an Indian chief, has maybe three to four hundred residents. It was incorporated two years after Olympia. It's further up the Sound so it will probably grow faster than your town. Excuse me, Mrs. Jewell; we have to get underway now." He knuckled his cap and turned toward the bridge.

I went back to the cabin to rouse my roommates and get the packing done. I didn't know how long it would take for the *Orbit* to make port but I sure would be ready, ready for the rest of my life whatever it might contain.

The knock on the door interrupted our busy morning. Jake stood in the doorway and I wished him a good day.

"I thought you might need some help getting your gear up on the deck. I'll come by and let you know when it's time. Ernie will help, too." He pushed back his black ten-gallon hat, looked at me with his quirky smile, and left.

"I think Jake, the rake, has met his match," said Zona with her special drawl. "In case you couldn't see it, honey, he's in love with you."

"No, he isn't, he couldn't be. A plain-looking widow like me doesn't rate his attention. Besides, being a widow doesn't mean I'm not married." I hoped she'd believe my words. I didn't want anyone, including Jake, to know the tremors he caused in me.

Bells clanged and I could hear feet running on deck. I went up into the companionway to see what happened. Sailors furled the sails as we glided into the port of Olympia. Jake appeared beside me. "It's some sight, isn't it?" he asked with awe in his voice. "It's been a long time since we hit the Cowlitz Trail to go get our engine."

"If my brother isn't here, is there a hotel where we can stay?" I asked

"Yes, a couple of them." He sounded so weary. "Ernie and I will get your baggage; you stay here and get acquainted with your new town."

Soon Zona and Lucy joined me on deck. "So this is Olympia, the territorial capital," Zona said. "I've seen worse and I've seen better." I felt again her resilience. This woman would land on her feet no matter what the circumstances.

I searched the road that led from the dock between the various buildings. I longed for the sight of a carrot-top but to no avail.

"Don't worry, honey, he'll be here. If he's late, you can stay with me at the Gold Bar," Zona said. She straightened her cap and pulled herself up with defiance.

I could see a group of men shouting to Jake and Ernie. They must be fellow firemen, their excitement palpable. My two fellow shipmates waved their hats and pointed with pride to the engine still lashed between the masts of the brig.

Jake and Ernie followed us down to the cabin to retrieve our baggage, the excitement a physical feeling for all of us.

Back on deck surrounded by bags and the few passengers, we embraced the views of our destination. The dirt street leading from the dock had one- and two-storey buildings along it in a haphazard manner. Several drays with horses between the shafts waited impatiently for cargo dispersal.

When I had about given up hope of seeing Andrew, the red-headed man appeared holding his little girl in his arms. Tears streamed down my face at the sight. It had been nearly ten years since I'd seen his strong features capped with that carrot-colored hair.

"Is that him, Mz. Hannah?" Lucy asked pointing to Andrew.

"Yes, Lucy, that's my brother. He looks so tired."

What this man had been through probably rivaled my past losses. I wanted to jump over the rail and hold him in my arms. Instead, I acted like the prim lady I was supposed to be and swallowed my impatience.

After we went down the gangplank with the other passengers, I looked up to see Jake watching me from the rail. He'd paused in the chore of freeing the fire engine from its restraining ropes to look at me. He saluted me with a touch of his hat, his lips lifted in a quirky smile and he turned away. Oh, how I wished our time together could have been prolonged. On the other hand, I knew it could lead nowhere.

Chapter Nine

Andrew hugged me so hard I couldn't breathe. "I am so glad you're here, Hannah," he said, eyes moist with unshed tears. He clutched his broad-brimmed hat in one hand.

"I'm glad, too, Andrew. We're all of our family we have left." Tears ran down my cheeks and I tried to brush them away but they kept falling.

Little Abigail hid behind her father's legs, peering around occasionally at the newcomer. "Are you Abigail?" I asked. She nodded and I went on, "How old are you, Abby?" She held up one hand with fingers extended and then the index finger on her other hand.

"You're six years old?" I asked. She smiled and her age was no longer in doubt because of the gap in her front teeth. "Did you put your teeth under your pillow so the tooth fairy would leave a gift?" She looked up at her father with doubt in her eyes.

"We don't have much so there couldn't be any gift," he answered my question.

He looked at something behind me so I turned to see my two traveling companions watching the emotional scene.

"This is Zona who's the new manager of the Gold Bar Restaurant and my companion, Lucy, from Ruby Acres. She's going to be Zona's helper at the restaurant."

"So you're Hannah's brother," Zona said reaching out her hand. "We've heard a lot about you and we'll see you around."

Lucy nodded her head, started to follow her new boss, and then turned toward me. "I hope I get to see you, Miz Hannah, and thanks for all you done for me." She, too, had to wipe at her tears.

"No more Miz Hannah, Lucy, we're friends so it's Hannah from now on. Of course we'll see each other, as often as I get to town."

A young man, leaning over a bit as if intent on his shoes, hurried up to me, an apron tied over his dark trousers and white shirt with a bow tie bobbling at his throat. "Are you the new manager?" he stuttered. Without waiting for an answer, he went on, "I'll help you with your luggage. Oh, I'm Arthur."

Since his remarks were aimed at me, I replied, "This lady is the new manager and I'm sure she'd appreciate your help," I said as I pointed to Zona.

Zona's knowing smile eased the young man's consternation and she indicated her array of suitcases and trunks.

"Oh my," he began. "Wait here while I get a wagon." He trotted off with his short steps, his eyes searching the ground through his thick glasses. One lock of black hair fell over his forehead.

Zona shook her head with resignation as if this were a commonplace occurrence in her move from job to job. While we waited, she said, "If things don't work out for you, honey, come see me." She gave me a quick hug then turned to look up Main Street where the busy little man hurried back pulling a cart.

"I guess we better get going out to the homestead," Andrew said. "I've already got my supplies. There's always so much to do out there, I don't spend much time in town." He gathered my bags and we walked up the street where a lone gelding stood tethered to the rail with a wagon behind him.

Andrew helped me into the wagon then picked Abigail up and lodged her in my lap. She stiffened at first but then started to relax against me. I looked back at the firemen and their new engine. Jake gazed at me rather than the engine, tipped his black hat with a salute then turned away. My heart seemed emptier than it had before I had met the west Texan on the ship. Would I see him again?

The trip to the homestead began up Main Street and I got a good look at the Gold Bar where Zona would hold sway. The lower floor looked like a storefront with rooms above. What an unlikely place for the territory's first legislature, I thought.

After leaving town, we wound around huge evergreen trees and through valleys filled with lush grass. The mist had gone and been replaced by weak sunlight. The horse seemed to know its way without any guidance from Andrew.

"How far is it to the homestead?" I asked.

"It's about five miles from town. We'll be there for the mid-day meal."

"I'm so glad my long journey is over. I don't think I ever want to take a sea voyage again." I tried to keep my back straight but it sagged with fatigue. Now that I had arrived, I could relax, I thought.

"Who was that guy in the black hat that kept staring at you?"

"That was Jake Buss. He's one of the firemen who went to New York to pick up the town's fire engine. He said it was the first one in Washington Territory."

"He sure had eyes for you, Hannah."

I just nodded not caring to discuss Jake with my brother. My feelings were too mixed up for an intelligent conversation on that subject.

Andrew turned off the main track and followed a couple of ruts into the deep forest. "This is part of my homestead," he said. "I wanted to leave some trees between me and the road for privacy." I nodded.

We came to a clearing and there stood a cabin among the trees that reached high into the sky. Stumps dotted the opening which gave mute testimony to Andrew's endeavor to carve out a farm in the wilderness.

The cabin's sides had upright logs and a stone chimney speared through the peaked shake roof. One window gleamed on one side and a door entered from the end of the structure. A porch protected the entry.

"It's not much, Hannah, but it's mine," Andrew said apologetically. "I know it's not what you're used to but I need you to help me so much." He choked with emotion.

"It looks fine to me, Andrew. For the last year, Lucy and I have lived in a slave cabin so this is a palace to me. You know I'll help all I can, Andrew. We were raised as workers, not drones. And what I left didn't look this good after the Yankees brought war to Ruby Acres."

"Well, let's get this stuff in the cabin and I'll show you where you and Abby will sleep. I'll spend the nights in the lean-to out back. The cabin has only one room. Mary hung a curtain across it making a bedroom in the back."

I helped with the unloading and Abby watched us work. The cabin had little furniture in it but enough to survive. There were two chairs and a stool, a small table, and cabinets on two sides of the kitchen area that sported a cast-iron stove. At least I wouldn't have to cook over an open fire.

Andrew started a fire in the fireplace to dispel the chill then left to tend to his livestock while I searched the cupboards for food.

After a meal of bread, cheese, and apples, we sat back and rested from our labors.

"You mentioned in your letter that you were going to find out what happened to John," Andrew said.

"I did try both at the Southern and Northern headquarters but to no avail. The North said he'd been a prisoner in a camp hospital and that an epidemic of typhoid had decimated the population in that camp but there were no records of who had died. They have my address in case they find John's records." I sighed with the feeling of futility.

"Were you happy in the South?" Andrew asked watching my face.

"I was happy with John, the love of my life, but his family didn't accept me and I lost patience with the futile existence of those southern belles. I was used to work and found it difficult to laze away the days. Actually after the men went to war, I kept Ruby Acres running until it was destroyed."

"That sounds like you, Hannah, always the rock. And just for the record, John wasn't good enough for you," he said firmly. "He just wasn't your type. It seemed to me he was all on the surface."

"I don't know about that. It wasn't as if I was inundated with male attention. One reason I loved him, I think, was because he loved me. He did his best, I'm sure, and I miss him." No tears this time for John.

"Now tell me about Pearl. Let's get all the sadness out of the way."

"She was bright, inquisitive, beautiful and loving. Her death devastated me more than John's because I couldn't save her. She died in my arms." Now the tears flowed.

"I'm so sorry, Hannah," Andrew said as he laid a hand on my shoulder.

"It's your turn, tell me about Mary. You married her out here so I never met her and you said little in your letters." I wiped my eyes and looked at him intently.

"She was pretty and small. We were both so happy when Abby was born. It was a hard pregnancy because Mary was somewhat frail. She tried to cope with life on the homestead but she'd been raised in town so it was a trial for her." He dropped his head in thought.

"How did she die, Andrew?" I asked softly.

"I really don't know what finally took her. She just wasted away, got weaker and weaker. She just had no energy to live; I guess; wouldn't eat, just lay in bed and died."

"So you had all the farm work to do, the housework to see to and taking care of Abby. What a load you carried." I said. "Well, you're not alone any more, Andrew, I'm here and I'll help shoulder the load."

Chapter Ten

Abby slept on a pallet in the corner and I plunged into sleep on the double bed behind the curtain that formed our bedroom. In a bed that didn't pitch and roll, I got a solid night's sleep and awoke refreshed, ready to make my mark on this wilderness.

Charging into the other half of the cabin, I coaxed a fire in the iron cook stove, started coffee and searched for the oatmeal. It had been a long time since I'd faced cupboards that were not bare.

Andrew must have smelled the brewing coffee because he appeared at the door, hair tousled and hiding a big yawn. One hand pulled up his suspenders. He picked up the wash basin, dipped some water into it and headed to the washstand on the porch. By the time he came back in, all neatly shaved and combed, I had Abby up and dressed.

We sat together at the small table eating oatmeal with delicious fresh milk and crunched on toast I had browned on the stove.

"What will you do today, Andrew?" I asked.

"Well, I have to burn the stump roots so we can pull them out. We need room for a garden so we don't have to go to town to buy vegetables. That's besides taking care of the cow, hogs and horse. The chickens just need to be fed and the eggs collected. Maybe you could do that with Abby's help." He wiped his mouth as he paused holding his spoon halfway to his lips.

"We'd like to do that, wouldn't we, Abby?" I said brightly. She nodded, not as enthused as I. "I really need to do some laundry, too," I added thinking of all the clothing that I had used aboard ship that needed to be cleaned. "How do I go about that? I saw the two wooden tubs hanging on the back wall but where does the water come from?"

"There's a small stream behind the lean-to. I'll get some water up here for you before I take care of the farm chores. Mary heated the water on the stove." He hung his head. Evidently he didn't like to talk about his loss. "When I get to it, I want to dig a well so the water is closer and with a pump it will be easier. That's in the future. I do have a barrel to catch rainwater. It's softer than the stream water."

"Abby will help me, won't you, dear?" Again she nodded half-heartedly. "Have you been to school, sweetheart?" I asked. She shook her head.

"As soon as you get up from your afternoon nap, I'll start teaching you to read. Would you like that?" No response.

With the day's schedule outlined, Andrew and I went about our chores. Abby's reluctance bothered me. "What's wrong, dear?" I asked. "Don't you want to help me?"

She looked down at her black stockings and scuffed shoes. "Mama didn't want me to do chores. She said she wanted me to be a lady and ladies don't dirty their hands." She looked up defiantly.

"Well, sweetheart, your mama's in heaven now and I'm here to take care of you. I believe every member of a household needs to do her share of the work. So, I'll wash the dishes and you will wipe them. Understood?" She nodded. I saw that my work was cut out for me in winning this child and helping her adapt to the life into which she was born.

The morning flew by as we did our chores and with an aching back I ushered Abby into the cabin to help get dinner on the table. When we completed our task, I used a wooden spoon to bang on a kettle calling Andrew in for the meal.

He carried a smoked ham with him and I cast a doubtful look at him. "Where did that come from?" I asked.

"I smoked it myself after butchering a hog last fall. I built a smokehouse and used some alder I cut down by the stream to smoke it. I thought we could have some for supper." Self-satisfaction suffused his face.

"That sounds wonderful, meat on the table." With decent food I might regain my sunny view of life even in this rainy country everyone told me about.

We sat at our usual places at the table and spent little time talking. When we finished, Andrew said, "Friendship with that Zona might not be too wise. You know what kind of reputation those women have and you don't want to be tarred with the same brush."

"Zona is a good friend and she's not one of 'those women'. She's the manager of the restaurant, not a madam. If it weren't for her, we'd still be in San Francisco," I responded vehemently.

"Okay, don't get upset. The Gold Bar has a saloon, too. I just wanted to protect you from gossip."

"I've dealt with gossip during my years in the South and I can handle it, Andrew. But I do thank you for caring." I gave a big sigh and thought again that life was never easy.

When Abby laid down for her afternoon rest, I went outside into the air smudged with wood smoke from the burning stumps. I gathered the dry clothes from the line, glad that the gray sky hadn't wept on my laundry. An hour later, the child came from her cot rubbing her eyes. "Ready for your first lesson?" I asked. She answered with an unenthusiastic nod.

As I taught her some words and how to sound them out, I noticed tears slipping down her cheeks. "What's wrong, sweetheart? Do you hurt somewhere?" I asked as I gathered her into my arms.

She hiccupped and murmured, "I miss my mama." Then she broke down completely. I held her for a long time until the sobs subsided. How sad for this poor child, bewildered at her loss and dealing with a new person in her life.

"It's okay to miss her and cry for her, honey. She's in heaven and watching over you although you can't see or feel her." I could tell this was a new concept for her and watched her face as she processed that information.

"Does she know you're here?"

"Yes, she does, and she sent me so I could care for you. I had a little girl just about like you but she's in heaven, too, with your mama." Now my eyes were damp.

"Would you like to help me bake some cookies?" She nodded and I thanked the powers that be for helping us past this big obstacle on the rocky shore of Puget Sound.

We developed a routine with Abby and I working in the cabin in the morning and then as she took her rest, I helped Andrew with whatever he did on the homestead. It felt good to do something positive and to contribute to the success of the homestead. Andrew seemed pleased with my efforts and told me time and again how much he appreciated my help, especially with Abby who warmed to me a little more each day.

As I pondered on how my life had changed, Andrew came into the cabin, his hand dripping blood. "What happened?" I asked in alarm and I grabbed a towel and wrapped it around the wound.

"The axe slipped and it hit my hand," he said as he sat down abruptly, hanging his head. I thought he might pass out.

"We have to get you to a doctor," I said. "Hold that towel tightly around your hand and I'll go harness the horse."

"You can't do it and I can't," he said weakly.

"Yes I can. I did it at Ruby Acres and I can do it here. Just hang on." I told Abby to get her coat and bonnet as I headed toward the barn.

With Duke harnessed and drawn up to the cabin, I helped both Andrew and Abby into the wagon and urged the gelding to move into the lane. He knew the way to town and all I had to do was give him a flick of the reins now and again to hurry him along.

I prayed I'd know where to go in Olympia. Zona was the only one I knew who would help and I instinctively felt she would be good in an emergency. Andrew's face had developed a ghastly look. Although he held Abby between us with his good arm, I could see his strength ebbed rapidly.

Smoke from a number of structures rose into the rainy sky so I knew we neared civilization. I pulled Duke up in front of the Gold Bar and ran inside shouting for Zona. The male patrons looked at me as an intruder but I didn't care. I needed help.

"Who's calling me?" Zona asked as she came down the stairs.

"I need help, Zona," I cried. "My brother cut his hand and is barely conscious."

Immediately she sent someone for the doctor and ordered two men to help Andrew through the restaurant into the saloon. She became the general in charge and everyone obeyed her without question.

A man dressed in black with muttonchop whiskers came into the restaurant and went through the swinging doors into the saloon with a black bag in his hand. He doffed his black hat and headed to where Andrew lay on two tables pushed together against the wall. "Stand back, now, and let me take a look," he said with authority.

I gathered Abby from the wagon, hitched Duke to the rail and went back into the saloon. I tried to remain calm for the child's sake. Zona took her from my arms.

"Please God, take care of him," I silently intoned as I watched the doctor. If the drinkers felt shock at seeing a woman in their domain, they didn't show it.

Chapter Eleven

With my head bowed I continually prayed for strength to cope with this latest catastrophe in my life. I felt a hand on my shoulder and thinking it was Zona, I rested mine on hers. I looked up and the comforting hand belonged to Jake. I quickly removed my hand lest he think I had special thoughts for him.

"You handling this okay, Hannah?" he asked still touching my shoulder.

"Of course; I can handle anything." I said with little conviction. How much was a person expected to endure in one's life? It was time for me to put my old Yankee determination into play.

I watched as a couple of men held Andrew and put a cup to his lips. I assumed laudanum had been added to the draught. The doctor waited for a few minutes then I saw him thread a needle so I knew my brother would have stitches in his hand. When the doctor finished his sutures, he nodded to the men holding the patient to the table and they stepped back.

Approaching the doctor, I asked, "How bad is it, doctor?" not sure I wanted to hear the answer.

"Fortunately, he didn't cut any tendons and the damage is to his left hand. It should heal nicely with a scar to show the ladies. It will just take time," he said as he turned down his cuffs and put on his black hat. He smoothed his whiskers and winked, "I'll send a bill out to the homestead. I might need a ham and maybe some fresh eggs."

"Can I take him home now?" I asked.

"As long as he has some help getting into the wagon. Keep the wound clean and use some of this ointment every day as you bandage it." He placed the small jar in my hand. "And here is some laudanum for his pain. Do you know how to use it?" I nodded and he left.

Jake stood by and heard all of the doctor's instructions. "I'll help get him in the wagon, Hannah, as soon as he's ready to go." He gazed into my eyes and I floundered in their depth.

"Thank you, Jake; I'll appreciate your help." I looked around for Abby in the restaurant. I glimpsed her on Zona's lap with Lucy peering over her shoulder. I went to them and Lucy hugged me a bit apprehensively.

"Are you happy here, young lady?" I asked watching her intently to divine if her answer were the truth.

"Oh, yes, Hannah. I'm happy with Zona and she's continuing my education where you left off. I finally feel I'm a free person." The bright smile of white teeth in her light brown face confirmed what she said.

I turned to the restaurant manager and said, "The only person I could think of to help me was you, Zona. I'm sorry if I upset things here."

"I'm ready to help you any time, honey, and don't you forget it. Anyway, the excitement is good for business. Look at the guys lining the bar." She laughed her hearty chuckle and stood, still holding Abby. "It looks like your patient is rousing. It might be a good idea to get him home. The boys will help."

I turned back to her and asked, "What's the doctor's name? I completely forgot to ask. I was so upset."

"He's Doctor Blake. Now he's a real rake," she answered me with a glint in her eye and a smile on her face.

A few men got Andrew to his feet and with their help he shuffled out to the wagon. Zona provided a blanket in the back to soften the boards and to enfold the man. I noticed Jake's absence when he had offered to help. I put Abby into the back with her father, unhitched the horse, thanked the helpers and turned to go back up Olympia's Main Street.

Clear skies blessed the trip home and we progressed at a much more sedate tempo than the careening ride from the homestead. I heard hooves moving up from behind us and angled the wagon toward the side of the road to let the rider pass. He didn't pass but kept pace with us. Jake honored his promise to help and I could not suppress the gratitude I felt for his support.

When I pulled into the yard next to the cabin, the sky lowered and I feared we wouldn't get Andrew into shelter before the rain began. During my short stay in

Washington Territory I had come to learn what the Olympians meant when they said it rained all the time.

We settled Andrew into a chair and I realized he couldn't sleep out in the lean-to with his injury and the cooler nights. I started toward his nightly abode to get his cot but Jake stopped me. "Tell me what you want and I'll do it. You take care of your brother."

I indicated the shed and asked him to bring in the bedding so I could make a pallet for Andrew on the floor. With the shock to his system, I thought my brother should be kept warm.

Jake soon brought Andrew's skimpy bed into the cabin and while I sorted it out he said, "I'll take care of the livestock," and left again. I saw him look up at the weeping sky as he settled his black hat more securely on his head.

It was impossible for me to equate the value of his help. Here I was with my injured brother who did the outside work and tended the farm animals, and dear Abby whose apprehensive looks and posture needed nurturing too.

When Jake came in with the milk and eggs I tried to express my gratitude. "I don't know what I would have done without you, Jake, even though you are a rake."

"You can forget the 'rake' part, Hannah. The name was a joke anyway. You know I will help you any way I can." he said with his laconic, twisted smile. "I could stand a little food, though, and I bet your family could, too."

Fixing supper gave me time to settle down and contemplate how long Andrew would be incapacitated. As soon as his left hand started to heal, I felt he could do quite a bit with his right hand since he was right-handed.

After I cleared the table, I looked at Jake. "I hate to see you riding into town in the dark. Why don't we fix another pallet here on the floor for you then you could do the morning chores before leaving?" Did I search for a reason to keep him here?

He looked intently at me and nodded with a light in his eyes and a small lift of his right lip. "Sounds like a plan to me, Hannah, good for both of us."

With Jake's bedding in place and having given Andrew his pain medication, Abby and I made our nightly trek to the privy before calling it a night. I found that the child was frightened to go out into the dark by herself so it became a ritual and helped our bonding.

As she and I settled into our beds behind the curtain, I could hear male voices murmuring in the other room. I drifted off to sleep wondering what the two men found to talk about.

Light filtered through the mist and the window the next morning. I roused a little. Still in the dreamy world between sleep and the real world, I thought about that intriguing man under the same roof, his talking eyes, his smile, and most of all his electric touch. How wonderful it would be to sink into his arms and let the rest of the world go by.

Abby stirred and sat up rubbing her eyes. Reality inserted itself and I put my foolish meanderings aside and I vowed not to let my dreams run away from me again.

Chapter Twelve

I made sufficient noise as I dressed Abby and myself the next morning so that the men in the other room knew we were about to invade their territory. As I pulled back the curtain, I saw only one man on a pallet, my brother.

"Has Jake left already? I wanted to thank him for all of his help," I said disappointed by his absence.

"He's gone out to do the chores," Andrew explained. "He's quite a guy. We got pretty well acquainted last night. He seems to think a lot of you."

I bridled at that remark but hoped my brother failed to notice. "I'll get breakfast started right away." Busy hands kept my thoughts at bay.

"He suggested we build a loft above the bedroom. That way I could sleep here instead of the shed. We talked about using the lumber from the shed. It wouldn't take much and he's willing to do it with my help. My hand hurts but that will get better. By the way, I need another shot of laudanum."

As I prepared his pain medication I reduced the amount of it worried about creating an addiction. "That would certainly relieve my mind, Andrew. I hated to think of you out there in all the wet and cold. I'd feel more secure, too. Is Jake going to stay here today? I need to know how many mouths to feed."

"I really don't know. I know he has a draying business to take care of but he'll tell us. It's a relief to have an extra pair of hands after my stupid accident. There's so much to do on the homestead, more than I can do one-handed and I don't have the money to hire help. I haven't the cash to pay the doctor either."

"You don't have to worry about that. He said a ham and fresh eggs would settle his bill. Food must be the frontier currency," I laughed. "After breakfast and seeing to the chickens, I'll dress your hand."

Jake came in just as I finished putting breakfast on the table. I hurried to take the pail from him and the eggs. I wouldn't have to check the chickens after all. The four of us sat down to our meal. Abby seemed curious about the new man but was too shy to speak.

"We were wondering if you're going to spend the day or if you have to get back to your business," Andrew said relieving me of the need to probe. I didn't want to seem anxious to have him here.

"I have a couple of hauling jobs today but I'll be back late this afternoon to do the chores," he smiled at me and my heart lurched.

"We'll expect you for supper, then, Jake, and you'll have to make up a bill for what we owe you," I said smoothing back my hair into its untidy bun.

"Don't worry about it, Hannah. People out here help each other when they can," he said, looking at me intently.

"Well, I hope you realize how much we needed you," I replied.

"I do, Hannah, I do, more than you know." He touched my shoulder, knuckled his hat to Andrew and left us. We heard his horse trotting away and we looked at each other.

"I don't know what we would have done without him," Andrew said with wonder in his voice. I agreed with him wholeheartedly but in silence.

The day stretched ahead and I kept busy to make the time pass more quickly. Andrew lodged his flat-brimmed hat firmly on his head and headed outside to check around the stable and get water from the stream that had grown in width with the fall rain. He had told me that most men around here wore a hat like his to keep the rain from going down their necks.

I straightened the house, did the dishes, fixed dinner, ushered Abby to the bedroom for her afternoon rest and then gave her a lesson after she awoke. During all of this activity I kept a sharp ear out for the sound of a horse. Finally, I heard one approach.

As I hurried to the window, I patted my hair in place and smoothed my apron over my calico dress. Disappointment awaited me. Doctor Blake in his dark suit, white shirt and ever-present flat black hat rode into the yard.

Andrew came from the stable to greet him. "Hi, Doc, what brings you out to my homestead?"

"I thought I'd bring my bill out in person and see to your hand." He alighted from his horse and tied her to the hitching rail along the porch. "Is your lovely sister around?"

Andrew gave him a calculating glance. "Yes, she's in the cabin. Come on in."

The doctor took off his hat and followed my brother inside. "Doc's here to collect on his bill, look at my hand, and to see you, Hannah," Andrew said with a gleam in his eye watching my reaction.

I smothered my disappointment and inquired pleasantly, "Is there something I can do for you, doctor?" I asked.

"No, ma'am, I just thought I'd like to know the Delaneys better. I like to welcome newcomers to town," he said with a bit of a smirk. I had to look down on the short man and noticed for the first time his slight paunch and thin mustache besides his sideburns.

"My brother's been here for some time, doctor, and my name is Mrs. Hannah Jewell. Please sit and I'll fix some coffee."

"Oh, then, is there a Mr. Jewell?" he asked as he settled at the table.

"There was. He died in the late war." I said with finality.

"Come here, Andrew, and let me take a look at that hand," the doctor stated. He unwrapped the bandage I had applied in the morning and studied the wound. "That's fancy stitching I did and it looks like it's going to heal very well. You did a good job of dressing it, Mrs. Jewell. I could hire you as a nurse," he simpered. "I'll just give you a little laudanum, Andrew." I watched the amount he used, more than I felt Andrew needed.

"I have too much to do here. I'm afraid you'll have to find another nurse." I poured his coffee and added, "I'll get your ham and eggs ready. You did say that was what your bill would include, didn't you?"

"Yes, ma'am, that would suit me just fine, and the next time you're in town, I'd like to take you to supper." He stroked his mutton chop whiskers with a glitter in his eye.

"The only time I've been to town since I've been here was our mad dash when Andrew cut his hand. Helping my brother is a full time job." I spoke pleasantly but without emotion.

"Well, the offer still stands, Mrs. Jewell. I think we would have a good time together," Dr. Blake said as he put his black hat securely on his head, smoothed his facial hair and went out the door to his mare.

Now there were two rakes in my life, a life that had contained only one man of importance before the war. As I hoped for the sound of hoof beats along the trail, I wondered how long I was supposed to grieve for a corpse.

Chapter Thirteen

My ears finely attuned to sounds from outside were finally rewarded with the jangle of harness and the clop of hooves. Afraid of disappointment again, I went to the window warily and saw to my relief that Jake drove a wagon into the yard behind a pair of prancing horses.

In the wagon's bed were two-by-fours and some other lumber. I went out to greet him and Andrew came from behind the stable. Both of us looked with wrinkled brows.

"Have you stopped on your way, Jake?" asked my brother.

"Nope," Jake said laconically. "This is my destination. I found some lumber we can use for the loft without tearing down the shed." He swung down from the wagon. His graceful movements impressed me again. "Can I bed down here again tonight?" he asked.

"You certainly can, Jake," I said too brightly. "You're our second visitor today."

"Oh, the fellows finding out there's an attractive unattached woman out here already?" he asked with a grin at me.

"No. Dr. Blake came to check on his patient," I answered curtly

"And to spark my sister," Andrew said with a laugh.

"I guess I ought to stake out my territory early," Jake said as he looked meaningful at me. "Let's get the lumber unloaded here by the cabin then I can unhitch the horses."

Andrew and I helped Jake unload the wagon. It didn't take long and soon Jake drove his team to the stable to unhitch them and I hurried into the kitchen to start supper.

The mere fact that Jake would be in our home again excited me and forced me to take a look at myself in the one and only mirror propped up on the kitchen cabinet. I smoothed my hair, washed my face and put on a fresh apron.

Soon the smell of cooking filled the small space and the men came in to eat with Abby and me. The child appeared to be more comfortable with our visitor this time since he'd spent the previous night here. She had been so shy since I arrived but seemed to be coming out of her shell. She even made a few remarks during supper.

"Wow, what a meal, Hannah," Jake said. "I haven't had vittles like that for a long time. You're a good cook, too."

I thanked him and wondered what else he found about me that was good. I admonished myself to forget this schoolgirl foolishness and behave like a mature widow.

After Abby and I finished the dishes, we joined the men around the fireplace. Sometimes the chimney gave off more smoke than heat in this rainy weather. Andrew filled his pipe and the aromatic fumes added a touch of hominess to the atmosphere.

They discussed the way they'd build the loft and I said, "I've got an extra pair of hands if you need them."

Again, I made the pallets on the floor then Abby and I made our nightly way out to the privy. When we came back into the cabin, the men left to take care of their bodily needs. Abby and I went into our chamber, readied ourselves for sleep, and climbed into our beds after saying our prayers.

I could hear Abby's whispers and went to her side and asked, "What did you say, honey?"

"I like that man," she said shyly.

"I do, too, Abby," I said to her and to myself I added, "very much."

It didn't take long to get the routine chores out of the way the next morning so work could begin on the loft. With an economy of movement Jake began with the rafters as Andrew cut the two-by-fours to the measurements already defined. My brother had asked for more laudanum but I was determined to wean him away from possible addiction.

After we placed the first beam, we set a ladder against it and that facilitated getting the rest of the supplies up where Jake needed them. In two hours, the rudimentary loft posed ready for the pallets. After Jake carried them up, I followed to make them ready for sleeping.

Following the morning's labor, I fixed our dinner and we all sat around the table eating and glancing up at the new construction with self-satisfied looks. We had all helped, even Abby.

After dinner, the men went outside and with Abby's help I cleaned the kitchen and the floor where the pallets had been. After the privation I had endured in the south, I should be so thankful for what I had now; family, a child to care for, enough food to eat and a warm place to sleep. These all nourished my body and my mind but not my emotional vacuum. Maybe that's why I felt such yearning for Jake's attention. It seemed silly in a woman my age but I acknowledged it to myself.

I watched Andrew and Jake poking at the still-smoldering stumps and talking about them. I wondered about the subject of their conversation. I also wondered if Jake would spend another night since suppertime approached.

The men came to the cabin door and I asked superficially brightly, "Do we have four for supper and for sleeping?"

"Afraid so, Hannah, hope you don't mind feeding me again," Jake said with his crooked smile and smoky blue eyes.

"Don't mind a bit, Jake. I hoped you'd stay so we could properly thank you. The loft is such a simple solution to a knotty problem."

After supper we all settled before the fire again and talked about Olympia, the town I was eager to know. "What about Indians?" I asked.

"Well, there was an Indian uprising in the territory during the mid 1850's but most of the fighting took place east of the Cascade Mountains. Nothing much happened here except the settlers were very cautious when strange Indians appeared," Jake said.

"I remember how scared Mary was that some red man was going to steal Abby," Andrew added. "Actually, we didn't see any Indians out here on the homestead except as they passed through."

"Olympia's quite a metropolis now," Jake said. "It's a natural crossroads with trails from the interior leading to Puget Sound. Also in the mid-50's Mr. Bettman built his department store, a little after Sylvester built the Washington Hotel. The first school at the corner of Sixth and Franklin collapsed under an unusual snowfall the first winter of operation and a new school went up at the same site. Now that's quite a history lesson for you," Jake added. "Oh, and the park you saw in town is the oldest town square in the territory."

"What about a newspaper?" I asked, always the avid reader.

"We have some of those, too. *The Columbian* I think was first published in the early 1850's and the first weekly in Washington Territory. Then we have the *Evening Olympian*, too" Jake responded.

I saw that Abby's eyes drooped so we made our nightly pilgrimage outside. When we came back into the cabin, Jake stood looking at my bed. "What in the world are you looking at, Jake?" I asked, puzzled by his presence in our chamber.

"Your bed sags. I'll tighten the ropes. It won't take a minute." He worked with the ropes knotting them tighter. "There, now, you can sleep tight, sweetheart."

Chapter Fourteen

With his last word ringing in my ears, I clutched the quilt to my breast wondering what it might mean. Was 'sweetheart' a word that came easily to him or did it have special meaning? I drifted off into a rosy haze listening to the low rumble of men's voices from the main room and finally the groan of the ladder as they made their way up to their pallets.

The next morning, the men were in front of the newly-kindled fire before I gathered my wits and joined them. "I'll have breakfast going in a minute," I said as I went back to get Abby started on the new day.

As we sat down at the table amid the smells of ham, eggs and toast, I asked, "What was all of last night's chatting about?"

Andrew replied, "Jake said as soon as the stumps have burned enough, he'll bring his team out to pull them. We'll really have a fire then. We could even roast potatoes." He grinned. It was so good to see the veil of weariness and sadness lifted from my brother's brow.

After Jake did the morning chores with Andrew's help, he hitched his matched roans and drove out of the yard without a backward glance. How I yearned to hear another endearment but that was not to be.

September flowed into October and as the temperatures headed down, the cold fall nights painted the vine maple leaves red and gold. They glowed against the lush green background of the tall firs that edged the clearing.

Andrew's hand healed quickly; after Jake's departure, he did all of the chores himself. He continued to burn the roots and toward the end of the month declared the stumps ready to pull.

"Let's go to town for supplies and to see Jake," Andrew announced one morning. "Make a list of what you need." He seemed expansive and I delighted in the thought of seeing other people. It would be good to visit with Zona and Lucy. I didn't admit to myself that the person I really wanted to see was Jake.

For the first time, I detected some enthusiasm in Abby. Her eyes sparkled and she chatted away as we completed our chores and got ready for the trip to Olympia. "Will we see the white-haired lady?" she asked.

"We most certainly will," I assured her. "And we'll see Lucy, too. She came with me from North Carolina and is a good friend of mine."

She nodded then asked, "Was she a slave?"

"She was, but not any more. She's as free as you and me." I put finishing touches on our attire and headed out to the wagon Andrew had pulled up to the porch. I could hardly wait to get to town.

The brisk fall weather brought roses to our cheeks and we made the trip to town in high spirits waving to those we passed on the way. Andrew pulled up in front of Rosenthal's store and tied the gelding to the hitching rail. "You girls go see your friends while I get supplies. I'll meet you at the Gold Bar then we can get your groceries," he said. "Maybe Jake will be there or at least someone will know how I can get in touch with him."

Abby and I strolled down Main Street. We looked in store windows, greeted those we passed with a nod and finally went into the Gold Bar Restaurant. I quickly looked through the swinging doors to see if Jake were in the saloon but disappointment filled me because I did not see him.

Lucy came rushing to me, grabbed me in a hug, and said, "I'm so glad to see you, Hannah, and little Abby too." She knelt down and put her arms around Abby. "My, child, you've grown since I last saw you. Are you learning to read, just like me?"

Abby lost her shyness and prattled on about reading, feeding chickens, gathering eggs, stump burning. I had never heard her string so many sentences together.

"Well, honey, you finally came to pay me a visit," Zona said in her whisky voice. "It's about time. Now let's go back to my parlor so we can chat." She motioned all of us to follow her and what Zona commanded, all of us did.

She had Lucy make some tea and got some cookies from a shelf then we settled back for a good talk. She told of her experiences in the Gold Bar. "Not much different from any of the other places I've managed but I like the people here a lot. They don't seem to be as judgmental as in some of the other places I've been. Running the restaurant has been a challenge but I thrive on challenge."

"Andrew has burned the stumps enough so that Jake can pull them now, he thought," I said. "Other than that, life is just a day to day experience on a homestead. You do your chores then it's time for bed."

"Jake's been out of town. Seems he had to make a trip back to Texas for some reason or another. A lot of people have missed him," Zona said.

I had, too, but I wasn't about to tell my friend.

Lucy responded to a knock on the door and the bartender told her that Doc Blake wanted a word with Zona. "Have him come in, Lucy, and thank you."

Doctor Blake, dressed in his usual black with a very white shirt, came into the parlor and showed surprise as he saw me. I knew instinctively he feigned the feeling. He must have seen me come into the restaurant and then into the parlor.

"Why, Hannah, how nice to see you. Are you in town for long?" He went on without giving me time to respond. "Remember we have a supper date one of these days."

"As soon as my brother comes for us, we'll be on our way back to the homestead. There's so much to do we can't spend a lot of time in Olympia," I replied

"A restaurant with a saloon seems an improper place for a lady," he replied. Why don't you come over to my office so we can talk?"

"No, thank you. I came to see my good friend Zona and my other good friend Lucy." I said the words with finality. "We three are very close."

I could see the doubt in his eyes as he evaluated the situation. "Well, if that's what you want, but I still want to take you to supper sometime."

"We'll see, Doctor Blake." I answered coolly and he left the parlor.

Arthur summoned Zona to handle some situation and I had a chance to talk to Lucy alone. "Are you comfortable here, Lucy?" I asked.

"Oh, yes, Hannah. I like being here very much. It's so much different than the south," she answered with enthusiasm.

"Has anyone put you down because you're colored?" I wanted her to be treated like any other Olympian.

"No, Hannah. I don't go out much except to go visit the Pacific Hotel. The manager is colored, just like me, although she was never a slave. She's helped me a lot, and of course Zona is a wonderful boss," Lucy emphasized.

My mind cleared concerning Lucy's experiences in this frontier town that didn't welcome colored people.

Just then Andrew came through into the parlor followed by the doctor who just happened to see my brother enter. "Hi, doc, you did a good job on my hand. Can't even tell it was a bad cut. You can barely see the thin scar."

"Do you need some more laudanum?" the doctor asked.

Quickly I replied, "No, we have plenty."

Andrew turned to me and said, "You ready to go get groceries, Hannah?" He turned to Zona who had just entered the parlor. "I understand Jake's been out of town. When he gets back, will you tell him I'm ready to pull stumps?"

"I sure will Andrew, and maybe Lucy and I will come out to your homestead to visit one of these days."

I nodded, hugged my two friends. Zona whispered in my ear, "Be careful of that doctor," and we left. I brushed by Doctor Blake without saying a word. For some reason I thought he faked his hearty manner without really feeling it. Maybe time would prove me wrong but that's how I felt now and his liberal use of the drug bothered me. And maybe the good thoughts were blocked by my feeling for Jake.

Chapter Fifteen

The trip to town had been a nice interval between chores but I couldn't begin to acknowledge how much I missed seeing Jake. That night in bed, my befuddled mind first conjured up John's image and then Jake's. Andrew had left word in town for the missing man to get in touch when he got back so the stumps could be pulled and the ground readied for spring planting.

Life continued on the homestead for all three of us except some of the joy had gone out of my perception of it. Churning the cream to make it into butter seemed to be the time I used to contemplate life in all of its aspects. The repetitive action soothed me and let my mind wander.

What would it be like to spend nights in Jake's arms and days waiting for his looks of passion and concern? He made me feel pretty rather than plain, a new concept for me. Unconsciously, I moved my hand over my tall frame. I straightened and continued pumping the plunger.

After I worked salt into the butter, I took the slops out to the pigs. Nothing went to waste on the homestead. I stood and watched the sow and boar root among the garbage. Today seemed a contemplating sort of time for me. I wondered why.

Just then I heard a scream from the house and raced to see what had happened to Abby. Andrew was right on my heels. I saw the child crumpled on the floor holding her left arm and sobbing. I ran to her, straightened her out and gingerly touched the left arm.

Andrew's alarm transferred itself to Abby so I cautioned him, "She's broken her left arm. It's a straight fracture so I can set it," I told him. "Go get two straight thin pieces of wood."

"I'll go get Doc Blake," he answered.

"No, do as I say. I've set many bones on the plantation so I know how. Get the laudanum from the top shelf in the cupboard for me."

He nodded, got the slats, and found the bottle of laudanum. For the fourth time, I wondered if an addiction had ended Mary's life. "Put a few drops in a cup of water and bring it here," I told my brother.

I put the cup to Abby's lips and she sipped the water. I waited for a few minutes until it started to take effect then splinted her arm wrapping the slats in a torn dishtowel. "There, that should do it. Pick her up gently and put her to bed." She seemed such a vulnerable human being with the loss of her mother, her father's cut hand and now a broken arm.

"How did it happen?" Andrew asked beside himself with worry.

"It looks to me she tried to climb the ladder to the loft and fell. She's been told not to do that but she's curious as most children are. She'll be fine, Andrew, really she will. She's only six and the young heal rapidly."

Abby spent a quiet night and the next morning seemed proud of her splinted arm. I fashioned a sling so she could move around without a lot of pain. I stayed in the house with her so she felt protected.

I heard a horse near the porch and looked out to see Andrew climb into the saddle.

"Where are you going?" I asked with alarm. "Is something wrong?"

"No, I just have to go into town. I won't be gone long," he answered and I heard the horse's hooves hitting the ground at a rapid pace. I wish he had confided in me and told me about his errand in Olympia.

An hour or so later, I heard his horse returning along with the sound of wheels. With Abby taking her nap, I went to the window hoping he'd found Jake but what I saw was the other rake. Doctor Blake got down from his wagon as Andrew tethered the team to the hitching post.

As the two men entered the cabin, Dr. Blake said, "I hear you have an injured young one here, Hannah. Andrew thought I should take a look at her and I welcomed the idea of seeing you, dear lady."

I hoped my fury didn't show. Obviously, my brother didn't trust my assessment of Abby's injury. I shrugged my shoulders and led him into the bedroom where Abby started to stir. "I've splinted broken arms before, doctor, and never had any complaints," I said stiffly.

"Those were no doubt slaves and this is a little white girl," he said smugly.

"The slaves and the little white girl are human beings and have the same appendages," I said.

He took a bottle of laudanum out of his case and started to prepare a dose of it for Abby.

"She's had a little of the drug but doesn't need any more. She's fine, aren't you, Abby?" I asked. She looked from me to the doctor and nodded her head leaning into me.

"Well, I'll just leave this here in case she needs some for pain later," the doctor said. "Her mother needed it and like mother, like child," he said with a sneering smile.

Instinctively, I knew the source of Mary's addiction.

Abby's arm healed very well and after a couple of weeks, the sling and splint were removed and I bandaged it tightly as the bone knitted. I'd been confined mostly to the house to watch out for her, admonishing her once again, not to climb the ladder to the loft. Silently I was glad to see her curiosity filling her agile mind. I felt all of those impulses had been stifled by her mother who transmitted her dislike of the pioneer life to her daughter.

Andrew spent these late fall days felling more trees to widen the clearing around the house. According to the Homestead Act of 1862, a homesteader had to be the head of a household and 21 years of age to claim a 160-acre parcel of land. Each homesteader had to live on the land, build a home, and make improvements and farm for five years before he became eligible to "prove up". A total fee of $18 was the only money required.

The importance of pulling the stumps hung on the horizon. If Jake didn't come back to town soon, Andrew would have to find another way. Time was of the essence because of the garden that needed to be planted next spring.

As I mulled these questions, I heard a horse trot up into the dooryard. I prayed it wasn't the doctor whom I really never wanted to see again. I looked out the window and my heart nearly leaped from my breast. Jake's lithe form swung from the saddle and Andrew appeared from the woods.

"So you're back in God's country, Jake. I'm sure glad to see you. When can you start pulling stumps?" Andrew held out his hand and Jake shook it warmly.

"This next weekend, I think. I have a lot of hauling to do this week but I should be clear by Saturday. I'll be here early. Will that work for you?'

"Fine, Jake, I really appreciate it. You could have sent word," Andrew said with a question on his brow.

"Well, I really need to talk to Hannah. Is she in the cabin?"

"Sure, come in." Andrew led Jake into the main room and I stood rooted to the floor. The sight of him chased all sorts of thoughts through my mind.

"Hannah, could we take a walk so we can talk?"

I turned a questioning look at Andrew who nodded. "I'll watch out for Abby. Go ahead and take a walk."

I gathered my shawl closely around my shoulders and Jake ushered me out the door. He put his hand under my elbow to guide me and the electric touch still shocked me.

We settled on the bank of the stream both sharing a large log. "There are a few things I need to tell you, sweetheart, and I hope you'll understand." He put his arm around my shoulder and I leaned into him.

Chapter Sixteen

Jake took a deep breath and said, "Hannah, you're the only woman I want in my life. I've loved you from the moment I saw you on that ship and never looked back." He kissed my cheek. I felt there was more to come and not nearly as affectionate as the kiss.

"For us to be together, you need to know why I was gone. Honesty is the only way I can see for us to be together. More than a month ago, I got a letter from a cattle baron in my home town. A couple of the other ranch hands had kept in touch with me so I guess he found out from them how to contact me.

"I punched cattle on his spread for some time and fell in love with his young daughter." He smiled a bit at the memory. "We'd go off into the hills, make love while the steers watched. We giggled about that. Anyway, we wanted to get married but the boss didn't want a cowhand for a son-in-law. He sent Julie away and nobody would tell me where she was."

Jake stretched his neck as if trying to clear his throat of unwanted words. "I couldn't stay there after that so I headed west. I thought it was all behind me and when I saw you, it faded into the distant past.

"This letter brought it all back with a vengeance. It seems Julie had a baby that my buddies didn't write about. She came back to the ranch for its birth but never married. I guess her father tried to force her into a marriage of convenience but she was as stubborn as her father.

"Julie died a few months ago and her father refused to recognize Jason, her bastard son, and wanted me to go get him or he'd send the boy to an orphanage."

When I gathered my wits, I asked with a sinking heart, "Tell me about Julie." I didn't move from within his arm.

"She was pretty and young. She was passionate and stubborn. She was my first love and I was young, too. I tried to marry her but her father had a lot more power than I did. I know how this must sound to you, Hannah. First love is so different than the mature love I have for you."

I tried to absorb all he told me testing each word for its veracity. I knew I had no right to this man but my inner feeling told me I wanted him. Finally I asked, "And what about Jason? Did you see him?"

"My first reaction was that the kid probably wasn't mine so I headed to Texas to prove someone else was the father." He looked at the gloomy sky, and continued, "When I saw him there was no doubt he was mine; same crooked smile, black hair, square chin." He smiled, "He's mine, alright, temper and all."

"Are you going to bring him back to Olympia?"

"I already have. My landlady's taking care of him. We got acquainted on our trip from Texas and he took to the hardships like a real trooper."

"I'd like to meet him, Jake." Children I could understand.

"I'll bring him along when I come to pull out the stumps this weekend. He and Abby could play together." He smiled, and then sadness entered his demeanor. "You know I love you, sweetheart. Is there any chance for a future together after this?"

"I'd be lying if I said I didn't care for you, Jake, but I have a lot of the past to overcome. Sometimes I feel I'm still married to John and other times I feel like a widow, free to do what I want."

"What do *you* want, Hannah?" he asked quietly.

"I want you, Jake." I paused, "but it will take a while for me to see my way clear for a loving relationship. Bring Jason and plan to spend Saturday night here." I leaned over, kissed his cheek and arose to go back to the cabin in great turmoil. I saw him put a hand to his face in wonder.

Saturday dawned clear and crisp, unusual for November I had been told. I got Abby ready for the day, fixed breakfast and we did our chores. Andrew had already gone to do his work getting all of the mundane responsibilities out of the way before the major work of the weekend.

Soon we heard the clop of hooves and two Shire workhorses drew Jake's wagon into the dooryard. Those majestic animals with such dignity knew their strength and condescended to use it for the good of man.

Next to Jake rode Jason looking apprehensively at these new people in his life. He crawled down and stood before us. "This is my son, Jason," Jake announced with his hand on the boy's shoulder. I could see the resemblance between man and boy and agreed silently with Jake that this was indeed his son.

"Have you had breakfast, young man?" I asked of Jason. He nodded. "Then I guess the men will get to work and we'll go into the cabin."

I took his hand, went over to Abby and told him, "This is Andrew's daughter, Abby. She's six." He looked at her with a small bit of shyness but that soon disappeared. This young man had cockiness about him even though he had lived only five years. The children were the same height and I had a hunch Jason had done a sight more living than Abby.

"Abby, why don't you take Jason into the bedroom and show him your picture books. I'll clean up in here?" I said after we went into the cabin. She nodded and soon I heard their young voices chattering to each other. It would be good for Abby to have someone her age about.

I looked out the window and saw that the men had finished talking about their strategy in pulling the stumps and piling them near the clearing by the stream. Those magnificent horses knew their role in the program and the pulling began. I found it hard to peel my eyes away from Jake and his fluid movements as he controlled those huge beasts.

I got on with my chores and soon dinnertime approached. I baked bread, fried ham, peeled yams and put squash into the oven to bake. Peeking into the bedroom I saw Abby reading to Jason who had a rapt look on his face, almost like it was a wonder that the girl could read.

When the food was ready to put on the table, I banged a pot with a wooden spoon to call the men from their labors. Andrew had made a couple of more stools so there would be enough seating for all of us at the table. I made the children wash their hands and we gathered for the noon meal.

"Will you be able to pull all of the stumps today?" I asked Jake.

"Most of them. We'll finish pulling tomorrow morning then start the fire." He tousled his son's hair with affection and I saw the look of adoration on Jason's face. I thought that Jake must have bonded with his son on the trip to the Northwest to have fostered that kind of feeling in such a short time.

The afternoon went as the morning had gone except I put the children down for their rest. Jason seemed reluctant but I promised I'd read them a story when they awoke and he finally succumbed on my bed while Abby slept on her pallet.

The fire in the fireplace needed more wood so I went out to replenish it and glanced at Jake who looked at me with a question in his eyes. I nodded and went back into the cabin with my arms full of wood. I stoked up the fire again, and sat in my rocker to contemplate a myriad of scenarios.

That rocker was special to me. Andrew knew of the chair-making mogul named Speak whose chairs were shipped by sea around the world. His business in Tumwater flourished. My brother had bought the chair for me when he had little cash. I took it as a gift of appreciation. I valued it and the sentiment that prompted his purchase.

When the children awoke, they came into the main room and sat before the fire with me as I read to them. Peripherally I thought that now I had children to care for, not just one little girl. My heart ached for the child I had lost but I reveled in the feeling of pseudo motherhood.

Supper repeated the gathering at noon and in the warm room the men talked about what they'd do the following morning. They went out to tend to the livestock while I made an extra pallet in the loft for Jason.

As the children's eyes started to droop, so did the men heave sighs of relaxation. Jake took Jason up the ladder to the loft after they'd made a trek out to the privy. Abby and I followed suit and the house settled into the night.

I had to admit to myself that I liked having Jake under this roof with me. If I could only feel confident that the past was really behind me, maybe I could look ahead.

Chapter Seventeen

How marvelous to wake up in the morning with loved ones filling the house. The thought astounded me but was right on the mark. The words, "God's in his heaven, all's right with the world," expressed how I felt.

Bursting with all sorts of energy, I bounded out of my bed, dressed, and went into the outer room to fire up the cooking range. I let Abby wake up and dress herself on her own. Today would be another great day in Washington Territory; I knew it.

Dawn painted the fog a rosy pink that told me the sun would soon be out to chase away the mist. I turned toward the window and screamed, then raced to grab the muzzle loader from the hooks above the mantle. Jake came hurtling down the ladder with alarm and asked, "What's wrong, sweetheart?" Andrew followed close on his heels.

"We're being attacked by Indians," I shouted as I pointed the gun at the window.

Both men laughed uproariously. Andrew said, "The Indians don't attack any more, dear sister," he said with tears streaming down his face.

"But his face was painted and he was staring into the cabin."

"They do that a lot," said Jake wiping his own tears of mirth from his face.

"And how much damage did you intend to do with an unloaded gun?" Andrew continued laughing.

I stared stupidly at the gun, at the window, and then at the two men who enjoyed my embarrassment. "Well, I guess I'd better get breakfast while you two comics get washed and I get the kids ready for the day."

When the laughter died down, Jake said, "It seems the Indians are curious about what goes on in cabins. They can stand and look in for hours. Most everyone around here has gotten used to it." He grinned.

The afternoon brought an end to the stump pulling and a great stack of them now poked into the sky near the stream. The weather had held so the pile of debris burned readily. When the time was right, I put potatoes into the coals to bake while I roasted a haunch of venison from the deer Andrew had killed a month before. I could barely look at the carcass as it hung in the shed. I wondered how anyone could shoot such a majestic animal with big brown beautiful eyes.

We sat around the supper table each of us feeling satisfied with work well done this weekend. I hadn't felt this fulfilled for a very long time. Teamwork had seemed a foreign concept in the South I knew.

"Well, it's time for Jason and me to hit the road to Olympia, I guess. It's been a wonderful time for us but I've got contracts to take care of now," Jake said as he arose.

"I don't know how I'll every repay you, Jake," Andrew said. "Now I can plow and be ready for planting in the spring. You're welcome here any time and for any length of time."

"I'll take you up on that, Andy," he answered as he looked at me. My heart fluttered like that of a young school girl.

We ushered father and son out into the dooryard where the magnificent draft horses waited patiently, already hitched to the wagon. Abby and Jason touched hands self-consciously then Jake heaved his son onto the wagon seat.

"If I see any marauding Indians, I'll send warning," Jake said leaving us with a laugh. My face flamed in embarrassment.

By late November, Andrew had finished the plowing and with that done, heaved a sigh of good work accomplished. Thanksgiving loomed, a national holiday proclaimed by President Lincoln in 1863. The celebration was fairly new but the tradition of the founding fathers of this nation still dictated the menu. I considered how we could find a turkey with all of the trimmings.

A young man astride a pony jogged into the dooryard. I recognized him as the young man from the Gold Bar who had helped with Zona's luggage. He hopped down from his mount, all business, and peered at me through his thick glasses as a hank of hair curled down over his forehead. "You're Hannah?" he asked with his nervous mannerisms.

"Yes, that's me. Can I help you?"

"Miss Zona sent this note to you and I'm to wait for a reply but I have to hurry back so if you could read it now and let me know your answer, I can go." He plucked at his sleeve and brushed back his hair.

The note invited the Delaneys and me to Thanksgiving dinner in Zona's parlor. She had invited a few guests and asked us to be among those whose company she wanted. I showed the note to Andrew, we looked at each other and he asked, "What do you want to do, Hannah? You've worked so hard here without any women friends. It's your decision."

The more I thought about it, the more I wanted to go. It'd be nice talking with other folks and getting to see more of the town. "Yes, I'd like to go, Andrew, and I think it'd be good for Abby, too." In the back of my mind, I knew Jake to be part of the equation and thought that seeing him in a different venue would be fulfilling.

"You're Arthur, aren't you?" I asked him. When he nodded I said,

"Tell Zona we'd be happy to join her for Thanksgiving."

"Fine, I'll tell her. You're supposed to enter the parlor through the rear door off the alley." He clambered up onto his pony and clopped down the road intent on his business.

Thursday's misty dawn leant an eerie feeling, almost supernatural, peaceful yet expectant. We started the day slowly savoring all of the things for which we gave thanks.

Andrew interrupted my introspection, "I'm especially thankful for you, Hannah. I was at my wits end after I lost Mary and if truth be told, some time before she died. Trying to take care of her and Abby besides proving up on the homestead nearly did me in." He hung his head and ran a hand through his mop of red hair.

"I'm thankful that you gave me a place to live and a way to be of some use, someplace where I am valued. No matter how much I did on the plantation, I was always the interloper and nothing earned me as much as a thank you." I shook myself. "I'm going to forget all of that and enjoy my new life."

"What about Jake?" he asked quietly

"I feel a strong attraction to him and he says he loves me but I'm torn between the past and the present. If I knew for sure John was dead, I could look forward to a life with Jake but there's this niggling doubt in the back of my mind. Maybe someday I'll be sure."

The trip into Olympia was one of joy. Excitedly, Abby posed all sorts of questions including one about Jason. "I don't know if we'll see them or not," I answered although I had mutely asked myself the same question.

Andrew dropped us off in the alley behind the Gold Bar while he went to the livery stable to house the horse.

I knocked on the door and Lucy threw it open. She drew us in amid the wonderful smells of turkey, dressing and pumpkin pies I saw cooling on the sill. Zona, abandoning her usual droll manner, enfolded me in her ample arms and said, "Welcome to my parlor, Hannah. You're my only real friend." Her whisky voice trembled with feeling.

"You're my only real friend, too, Zona. We're an unlikely pair aren't we? You a restaurant and saloon manager and me a homesteader." We hugged with true affection.

"And here's Abby. My you've grown since I saw you last. Your Aunt Hannah must be feeding you well," Zona remarked.

Abby's shyness had virtually disappeared and she said, "She's teaching me to read, too. I read to Jason."

"Is that Jake's boy?" asked Zona knowing the answer.

"Yes, he's younger than me but we're the same size. Hannah said she'd teach him to read, too," answered Abby pushing back a stray hair into her braids.

"That's good to hear. Maybe Hannah should be a teacher. She taught Lucy to read, too. Now, let's get your coats off and settled into my parlor."

The other guests appeared one by one including Jake along with Jason and Doctor Blake. I had never met the other man crowned with black hair sporting wings of white at his temples. I looked at Zona with a question in my eyes.

"This is the owner of the Gold Bar, Walter Anderson," Zona introduced as she noticed my hesitancy.

"I'm glad to meet you, Mr. Anderson," I said.

His courtly bow surprised me in this frontier town, "I'm glad to meet you, too, Hannah. Let's cut out the formalities, shall we? I'm Walt."

While the others chatted and laughed, I helped Zona set the table. For a moment we were alone and I asked in a sotto voice, "What did you mean when you said to watch out for the doctor?"

"He's not what he seems," she replied. She looked around to see who might be watching us then continued. "I have a feeling he gives people drugs and then when they can't do without them, he's the supplier."

"I came to a similar conclusion about Andrew's wife. What I couldn't figure out was why. Certainly the Delaneys had no money. I don't know about his other addicts."

"Maybe it's power he's after. Anyway, honey, watch yourself," Zona said as we made ready to enjoy this Thanksgiving feast and good friends.

Chapter Eighteen

The warmth wrapped us on our homeward journey. Abby slept in my arms, a satisfied smile on her cherubic face. The only discordant thought for me was the way Doctor Blake had hovered over me, as if he owned me. I had tried to elude him but found no way to do so without causing a scene to spoil the day.

Jake's speculative gaze made me wonder if he sensed my turmoil or if he thought I had some attachment to the doctor. I'd shoot him looks of despair but it seemed he couldn't read the message I sent.

I wondered if the new man, Walt, had a special place in Zona's life. She certainly deserved one. Of course, he was her employer so his invitation to dinner was legitimate without special overtones. The looks he gave her were beyond those of an employer, I decided.

We rolled into the dooryard and Andrew helped me down from the wagon before he unhitched the horse and led Duke to the barn. We still had chores to do; they didn't wait on weather, lethargy, fatigue or any other human conditions.

As I waited for sleep, I wondered why Jake hadn't spoken much to me, or to anybody for that matter. Maybe caring for his son took too much of his time between draying jobs. The disappointment of not being alone with him told me just how much he meant to me.

November rolled into December on cold winds and weeping skies. And then one Saturday, rare sunlight lit up the sky and gilded the fir branches. What a glorious sight. It lifted my heart.

In mid-morning, the sound of wagon wheels invaded my senses and I went to the window to see the source. Jake and Jason rode up and my anticipation soared, along with the sun.

Jake jumped down from the wagon seat, tethered the horses and strode to the cabin. I opened the door to greet him. "What brings you to the Delaney homestead this fine Saturday morning?" I asked in a facetious manner.

"Well, I have a light load to deliver out north of town and I wondered if the Delaneys and Mrs. Jewell would like to ride along, maybe even fix a picnic lunch." His quirky smile made my heart flutter.

"The Jewell part will fix a basket while you ask the older Delaney if he wants to go along. Come on down, Jason, and look at picture books with Abby while I get the sandwiches started." He needed no further invitation.

Andrew declined the invitation but Abby and I were eager to go. I left food for my brother and cautioned him not to work too hard while the rest of us played.

We started off with a brisk canter, the children in the bed of the wagon and I on the seat with Jake. He'd turn and smile at me once in a while as we made our way toward town. We stopped at the livery stable established by Edmund Sylvester on the northwest corner of Main and Third streets. It was the end of the line for all overland stages from Cowlitz Landing. Jake dashed into the office, came back with a large package, and we were on our way again.

The amazing sunny day held and we laughed, sang and waved to bystanders as we left Olympia headed north. "Where are we going?" I asked.

"Out beyond St. Joseph's Catholic Mission at Priest's Point to the Anderson homestead, Ernie's folks."

"I didn't know there was a Catholic Mission here. How interesting," I said, my curiosity working overtime. "And what is Priest's Point?"

"It's a point of land on Puget Sound. That's where we'll have our picnic." He urged the horses to move faster as if anxious to deliver his package and get back to the mission.

On the way back to town we angled away from the road toward the Sound on a lightly-used track. I saw a large, dark monastery surrounded by some Indian huts in the area. They all seemed in a state of disrepair. Jake explained, "Father Ricard started the mission in the 1850's and it was abandoned in 1860, so I'm told. He ministered to the Indians but was a force in Olympia, too. He deeded a portion of the land for a steam sawmill. It's run now by Carrick Crosby, Sr."

"How fascinating," I enthused. "Can we see the water from here?"

"We can stand on the bluff on the other side of the mission and see the Sound. I thought we'd take the trail down to the water to have our picnic. The kids can play in the sand while we relax and talk."

We started down the trail, hand in hand, trailing the exuberant children. Tall fir trees shaded us as we followed the well-worn track. We came to Budd Inlet, the lower end of Puget Sound, and looked across at a few dwellings nestled in the evergreen trees.

"I didn't know there would be houses across there." I pointed them out to Jake.

"That's what they call Marshville after Edmund Marsh whose land claim encompassed much of the land over there," Jake explained.

"Well, you watch Jason and Abby while I lay out our picnic," I said as I spread a blanket on the beach and started pulling food out of the basket.

After the feast, Jake and I watched the children play in the lazy sunshine. The man beside me lay quietly on the blanket and I basked in his nearness. He didn't speak for a long time and I thought he slept.

"Hannah, Doctor Blake is telling around town that you and he are going to get married and that you will help with his practice," he said solemnly. "Your life is your own, of course, but since we have no formal understanding, I am at a loss to know what's true and what's Doc's selective memory." He kept his eyes closed but I knew he waited for my answer.

"The man is greatly mistaken if he thinks I'd have anything to do with him or his practice. Do you know what his practice is?" I said furiously.

"He's a doctor. What else?"

"He dispenses laudanum unnecessarily then when he gets his patients hooked, he's their supplier. I know it's not for money but Zona thinks it's for power," I said indignantly.

"He hovered around you on Thanksgiving so I thought there might be some truth to his boasting," Jake said

"Jake, surely you know me better than that. Maybe you ought to look inside this packaging you see to the real Hannah." I steamed, I was so angry.

He turned over and looked straight at me. "Give me time, sweetheart, I'll find the real Hannah. I love you and I want to marry you," he said with his heart in his smoky blue eyes.

"I'll give you all the time in the world, Jake. It's you I want, not that slimy doctor." I sealed it with a kiss to his forehead.

Our trip back to the real world was warm with sun and emotions. The children, exhausted by their playing on the beach, fell asleep in the bed of the wagon.

Chapter Nineteen

We were well into December when the realization hit me that Christmas was just around the corner. I wanted to make it special for Abby and for my brother. I thought this would be the first happy Christmas for all of us after our devastating losses. I decided we should invite Jake and Jason along with Zona and Lucy. Andrew agreed.

We went to Olympia to get supplies for the great event. Abby and I could make paper chains out of red and green for the tree. That wouldn't be too expensive and since Andrew had sold some logs, there were a few extra dollars. While my brother got his supplies and the items I had listed, I went into the Gold Bar to invite our guests who were there.

Doctor Blake sat at a table in the bar, playing poker. He excused himself when he saw me go by and caught my arm. "I'd like to take you for dinner at the Pacific House, Mrs. Jewell. I was just about ready to go. Do come along."

I thought this would be a good opportunity to let the officious doctor know exactly how I felt about the rumors he'd spread around the town. "Fine, just let me leave Abby with Zona and I'll be with you."

She welcomed us with open arms as did Lucy who had blossomed so much in self worth. "I came to invite you both for Christmas dinner. I do hope you can make it and if Walt would like to join us that would be just fine."

"Without even thinking about it, we'd like to come," Zona said with Lucy's nod of approval.

"Wonderful. Now, if you'd watch Abby for a few minutes, Doctor Blake wants to take me to dinner. It's about time I set him straight," I said with determination.

"Sure thing, honey, be firm. He needs to have his ego deflated," Zona said with a sly smirk.

I left Zona's parlor and told the doctor I was ready to go. We strolled down to Main and Third and entered the building. The man had tried to take my elbow and I jerked away.

When we settled at a table, a waitress came along to take our orders. The doctor ordered a full meal and I asked for tea. "Is that all, ma'am?" the waitress asked.

"Yes, that's all," I replied.

"Now, my dear, you must have a decent meal," Doctor Blake said oozing charm, he thought.

"I won't be here long enough for a meal," I said, again with determination.

"You know, the Pacific House is a popular gathering place for Olympians and visiting legislators. Aunt Becky took over in 1860. Her real name is Rebecca Howard and she's a great cook." He put his hand over his mouth and whispered with a conspirational leer, "She's colored, you know."

"Skin color means nothing to me," I said. "We're all human beings."

His meal came and my tea.

I began, "Doctor Blake, it seems you've been spreading around town that you and I are to marry and that I'd help with your medical practice. I have never said I'd marry you and, if you were to formally ask me, my answer would be negative. As far as I know, I'm still married since there is no record of my husband's death."

"My dear lady, I'm sorry if I misinterpreted our relationship. You're such a fine woman; I thought you would be perfect for my wife. Maybe I got carried away."

"You thought wrong and I wish you would let others know you were mistaken." I sipped a little of my tea and added, "Thanks for the tea. Now I have to go get Abby so we can finish our shopping then get back to the homestead." I left without a backward glance. I hoped that would end the matter.

Christmas Eve arrived and most of our preparations had been completed. The three of us sat around the fire without lamplight. The feeling of satisfied endeavor filled us as we looked at the decorated tree in the shadowed corner. It was not elaborate but it suited our home and our circumstances.

Andrew had made benches for the table he had lengthened. Abby and I had fashioned the paper chains and draped them around the fresh fir tree my brother had cut and mounted on a stand. The aroma of apple pies with their rich cinnamon flavor filled the cabin. All seemed to be well in our little world.

On the great day, we three bounced out of bed early eager for the day to begin. Andrew had bought each of his women a bauble. I had knitted socks for him and a cap for Abby. We opened the gifts filled with the warmth of love they contained.

With a quick breakfast out of the way, I began dinner preparations. A big ham went into the oven wrapping us in its delicious smells. We did our chores with dispatch and waited for our guests to arrive.

Wagon wheels sounded on the track and we rushed out onto the porch to welcome our Christmas guests. Jake and Jason sat on the seat of one wagon while Walt drove a surrey with Zona and Lucy as his companions.

Confusion reigned for a while but eventually it was time for the big dinner. Abby and I had already set the table so I pointed out where each person was to sit on the benches and stools. Needless to say I seated Jake next to me. I had put a board across Abby's cot for the children's table.

Andrew carved the ham and I dished up the rest of the meal. We didn't stand on much ceremony and dug into the festive repast. As we finished the main meal, ready for the apple pies, I saw an Indian face in the window. They all followed my glance.

"Shall I get the blunderbuss for you, Hannah?" Jake asked with his quirky smile.

"I know you're making fun of me but that's fine, Jake." I got up, fixed a plate of food and took it outside to the Indian. I thought the gesture appropriate since we all inhabited the same space and sharing was part of the season's joy. I came back into the cabin with a satisfied smile on my face. "There, no firearms needed."

We sat around the fire patting our full stomachs and telling stories of past Christmases. "I remember one from a long time ago," Zona said. "I was in this godforsaken town with little more than a general store and the saloon I managed. All the miners were crying in their beer about not being with family at Christmas. I was about to tell them to go home if that's where they wanted to be. About that time, a young man and his wife came into the saloon, she large with child. The short version is that she gave birth there in the saloon with a whole room of godfathers. It was very special."

That topped all the other stories and when we looked out the window, we saw that snow fell gently adding a special feeling to the day. As our guests got ready to brave the dark and the snow, Jake pulled me aside and handed me a package. We had said there were not to be any gifts so I looked at him with a question on my face.

"Jake, I didn't get you anything. None of us can afford Christmas gifts."

He said, "Open it, Hannah. It's not really a Christmas gift."

I opened the package, removed the tissue and found a beautiful little ring with a diamond set into a gold band. I looked up at him with awe in my face.

"Will you marry me, sweetheart," he asked quietly.

"As soon as I feel I can, I will, Jake, my love," I responded.

Chapter Twenty

Jake's proposal kept me warm all through the first two months of 1867 while the wind blew and the rain lived up to its reputation in the Puget Sound basin. It drizzled, it poured, it misted, and fell gently displaying the sky's variety of precipitation.

Much of my thoughts centered on my answer to Jake. I had an obligation to Andrew and Abby as well as sheltering a doubt about John's death.

At breakfast one morning, Andrew asked, "What are you going to tell Jake?"

"I will marry him but only when I think it's right. You need me here right now and when I feel that John is truly gone then I can make plans about the future," I answered as best I could. "So I guess you're stuck with me for a while." I smiled.

He patted my face and replied, "Thank you, Hannah. I worried Abby and I would be alone again."

Early in March, Jake drove his rig into the yard pulled by his magnificent pair of draft horses. He and Andrew were going to do the final work on the plot designated for a large garden. Beside him rode a comely woman, small of stature with dark hair pulled back into a bun with Jason in her lap. The green-eyed monster sat on my shoulder as I tried to assess this newcomer. I asked myself if she were from the past or lodged in the present.

Jake helped her down after he had lifted Jason from her lap. "Andrew and Hannah, this is my landlady who watches out for Jason when I'm busy. Phoebe, meet Andrew and Abby Delaney, and the light of my life, Hannah Jewell."

"Welcome to the homestead, Phoebe," I said with relief as I reached for her hand. "Come along inside while the men get to work." I shuffled the children into the bedroom where they could play and look at picture books. Abby liked to act the part of teacher as she showed Jason how to recognize some words.

"I'm a widow, too," Phoebe said in a very quiet, low voice. "I lost my man in a logging accident. We had no children so I started taking in boarders to survive. It's worked out pretty well but I wish I had children. Jason is a good substitute but I'd like one of my own."

"My husband didn't come back from the War Between the States and I did have a little girl but she died, too. That's why I came out here to care for my brother's daughter. It's been a healing experience," I explained.

We continued to chat about a number of things and I found her to be an educated woman with some fire beneath the quiet exterior. We eventually took the children out to watch the men with those beautiful giants as they prepared the ground. I noticed that Andrew could hardly keep his eyes on his work as he cast furtive glances at Phoebe.

Phoebe and I prepared the noon meal and banged on a pot to call the men for dinner. With the longer table Andrew had made, we had enough room to be comfortable. I noticed my brother took special care in washing up and slicking back his red mop.

At the end of the day, a feeling of satisfaction of a good job well done filled us and love warmed me when Jake put his arm around my shoulders. "Does it suit you, sweetheart?"

"Oh, yes, Jake, I'm eager to help plant the garden. It's been a hard journey for Andrew but now there's a good future for him to look forward to." I smiled up at him.

"Speaking of futures, did you catch the way Andrew looked at my landlady?"

"Of course, how could I miss it? I think you had an ulterior motive in bringing her out here," I said awaiting his rationalization.

"Well, I thought if your brother took a liking to Phoebe, maybe that would eliminate one hurdle in our path to matrimony," he said with that heart-wrenching quirky smile that usually undid me.

"For Andrew's sake, I hope your ploy worked," I said, and then mumbled, "for my sake, too."

The next morning with breakfast out of the way, I followed Andrew out the door while Abby collected the dishes from the table. "Do you think we could cordon off a small portion of the garden for Abby, so she could have it for her very own?" I asked. "It would make her feel so much more a part of the homestead if she had her own space."

"Sure. I should have thought of it myself. I'll mark it off now and you can tell her," Andrew said as he clapped his flat hat on his Irish hair.

"No, you tell her, as father to daughter. That's the way it ought to be," I replied and went back into the cabin to finish with the inside chores so we could all help with creating the garden.

The weather turned balmy toward the end of March. It still showered but the warm rain helped our garden to grow. How excited we all were when little green shoots started to dot the dark soil. Abby jumped up and down when she saw her garden sprouting. In less than a year, she had changed from a shy, withdrawn and somewhat rebellious little girl to a partner eager to help. She no longer talked about her mother who had wanted her to be a lady with clean hands.

After our noon meal, I cleaned the kitchen ready to continue weeding the garden when I saw Jake ride into the dooryard leading another horse. He had abandoned his wagon for this trip. I went out to greet him with joy in my heart.

"What brings you to the Delaney homestead this fine day?" I asked.

"I want to take my lady riding," he said as he tethered the two animals to the rail and kissed my cheek.

"And where might you take your lady?" The light banter pleased me.

"I want to show her a few things. Do you think the Delaney family could spare you for the afternoon? I'd have you back in time for you to feed them supper." We strode toward Andrew and posed the question to him.

"Sure, go ahead, Abby and I will finish the weeding then maybe take a walk around the homestead." He wiped the sweat from his brow. "How's Phoebe, Jake?" he asked in an off-hand manner as if the answer mattered not.

"She's just fine, keeps asking about the Delaneys. I'll bring her out soon. If the rain lets up maybe we could have a picnic," Jake replied.

The second horse had a woman's saddle. I had learned to ride at Ruby Acres and although I preferred to ride astride, I could handle side saddle to preserve my modesty.

"Where are we headed, young man?" I asked lightly.

"That's for me to know and you to find out, as they say," he answered. "First, I want to show you a fine sight."

We rode in silence, enjoying the nearness of each other and the balmy weather that breathed a relief from the ever-present rain and mist. He took me on a few Olympia side roads then stopped in front of a palatial home that seemed too grand for this frontier town. The front steps led up onto a porch flanked by three pillars supporting a second-floor veranda. The wing to the right had two large windows with duplicate pillars on each side and another pillar between them.

"What a lovely home," I breathed. "Do you know the owners?"

"Daniel Bigelow, a lawyer, built it in 1860. He was one of the 54 people who signed the 1852 petition to establish Thurston County. He was elected the county's first treasurer."

"That's a mighty fine monument to him," I said. "Thank you for bringing me here and I enjoyed the ride." I turned my horse's head for the return trip but Jake took hold of the bit.

"The tour isn't over yet," he said. "We'll ride out past Priest's Point. I have something else to show you."

Chapter Twenty One

As we rode past Priest's Point, I recalled the wonderful picnic we had shared with Abby and Jason. The warmth of that episode filled me with a rosy remembrance. "Where are we going, Jake?" I asked. For some reason I thought the point was our destination.

"We'll be there soon," he replied mysteriously.

Maybe he wanted me to meet some of his friends who lived out here. The countryside was lovely with grassy stretches surrounded by those beautiful evergreen trees. The weather had cleared enough that I could see majestic Mount Rainier with its snow gleaming, a cap of clouds on its peak.

"The old-timers say that if the mountain has a cap, it will rain within 24 hours," Jake offered. "Of course, in this country that's a pretty sure bet without the cap."

We soon came to a trail leading through a stand of fir and cedar that continued for a mile or two then into a clearing where someone had started a cabin.

"This is it," Jake said. "I filed for a homestead some time ago so I've been working out here when I could take the time. I've started our cabin yonder as you can see. I wanted to show it to you so you could make any suggestions before I went any further."

"I'm breathless, Jake. It's such a surprise. You know I can't marry you for some time," I said but was thrilled nevertheless.

"I know, sweetheart, but I want our home to be ready when you are." He helped me down from the horse and held me in his arms. We kissed passionately for the first time and there was no doubt in my mind that this was my man and I was his woman.

We strolled over to the outline of the cabin and talked about size, rooms, and windows all the while remembering that moment when we really had committed ourselves to each other.

On the Delaney homestead our days were filled with nurturing the garden, caring for the livestock and widening the open space around the cabin. The stream nearly overflowed its banks from the heavy rain but didn't really threaten us. Jake appeared now and again keeping me abreast of the progress on our homestead. Occasionally he'd bring Phoebe and Jason with him much to my brother's unvoiced delight.

On his latest visit, Jake told us about the dance the fire department planned as a money raiser for the structure they wanted to build for a town hall and to house the Columbia fire engine. Agitation for support of the project had barely begun and the social would kick off the drive for funds.

"Will you go with me, Hannah?" he asked after telling us all of the details.

"I'd love to go, Jake, but I really don't have anything to wear except old, darned gowns." I looked down at the patched dress I wore. Presentable clothing was not a high priority on a homestead.

"Why don't you go to town and find yourself a party dress and I'll pick up the tab, sweetheart?" Jake proposed.

"Oh, I couldn't do that, Jake, not yet anyway. Let me think about it for a while."

Andrew listened to this exchange and said, "Maybe Zona would have something you could wear or maybe you could make a dress yourself. We'll go to town and see what we can find."

After Jake had left, Andrew and I sat at the table with fragrant coffee before us. "Hannah, do you think Phoebe would go to the dance with me?"

"If the way she looks at you is any indication, I'm sure she would. She's so lovely and amenable." It appeared to me he was asking more than just about the dance.

"She'd be a fine catch for you, Andrew, and a great mother for Abby," I said testing his feelings.

"I'd already thought about that, Hannah. You're very perceptive, I've found, just like when we were kids. You always knew what went through my mind," my brother said with a twinkle in his eye.

"So, when do we go to town, brother dear?"

"Everything is in good shape here so how about tomorrow?"

"Sounds just right for me," I replied.

As I entered the Gold Bar looking for Zona, Dr. Blake came from the bar through the swinging doors and gave me his oily smile. "You're just the person I wanted to see, dear lady. I've heard about the dance and would be delighted if you'd be my partner."

I could barely tolerate this man and answered with aplomb, "I'm sorry, doctor, but I'm going with Jake Buss. His invitation preceded yours." I didn't like the man but I thought it prudent not to antagonize him either.

Zona came out of her parlor to hear the exchange. "Hello, honey, come on in for some girl chat," she said with warmth and a smile as big as Texas.

We hugged and Abby went to Lucy where the two of them became engrossed in Lucy's reader.

"Jake has invited me to the firemens' dance at the end of August and I don't know what to wear. I've made do with the dresses I came with but none of them are suitable for a dance. Where could I go look for one that's not too expensive?" I asked.

"Look no further, honey, I've got a closet full of gowns that I've outgrown. We're of a height but I have put on an inch or two around the middle. After we have some girl talk, we'll have a look."

"I guess you know that Jake asked me to marry him. I told him I would when I could. I meant when Andrew had a wife and I felt that John was really dead," I said feeling the weight lift from me a little by sharing with my only good friend.

"There's no doubt in my mind you love him, Hannah, and he loves you. It's about as secret as the weather. Is there any candidate on the horizon for Andrew's wife?"

"As a matter of fact, there is. It's little Phoebe, Jake's landlady. When they're within ten feet of each other you can feel the sparks shoot between them," I told her with enthusiasm.

"Just like you and Jake, honey. You'd have to be blind and numb not to notice that you two are made for each other. If your brother and Phoebe get together, the only other obstacle would be how you feel about John." As usual she had cut directly to the heart of the matter.

"It's so hard, Zona, I know now that what I felt for John was more gratitude than love. No man had paid any attention to me to speak of. I'm taller than most women and plainer than most, too. I was thrilled that this cultured southerner chose me." I thought back to that time and felt mostly pain at what I had left in the south, primarily my little girl. For some reason, John had lodged in the back recesses of my mind.

"How long do you think he'd want you to wait until you formed a new life? You're a young woman, Hannah. I'm sure he wouldn't want you to go on alone forever if he was any sort of decent man," Zona said as she patted my hand. "How long do you expect yourself to wait?"

"I keep hoping some inner instinct will tell me when I've waited long enough. It's been nearly three years since I've heard anything from him or about him," I said.

"Don't you think that's long enough, honey?" Zona said quietly.

"Maybe it is, Zona, my friend, maybe it is."

"Time to look at my wardrobe," Zona said as she pulled me to my feet.

I found a gown that fit me and the style suited me to perfection.

"Thank you, dear Zona, for the dress and for your special friendship. I needed to talk to you so much," I said as I hugged her.

"Any time, honey, any time," she replied.

Chapter Twenty Two

Excitement filled the little cabin by the creek as Andrew and I got ready for the dance. Jake would bring Lucy to watch the children on the homestead and we'd go back to Olympia with him.

The dress Zona had given me had me preening before the cracked mirror above the kitchen sink, trying to see it from all angles. I took special care with my hair twisting it into an elaborate bun with curly tendrils before my ears.

Andrew took the same care with his preparations. I'd never seen him so concerned with the way he looked. It didn't take a scientist to know he wanted to impress Phoebe.

We planned to spend the night at Phoebe's rooming house and come back to the homestead in the morning. What a gift, to have the whole night away from responsibilities.

Having Lucy stay with the children eased my mind about leaving them. I knew just how dedicated she was to whatever task she undertook. Phoebe had come along, too, all dressed ready for the dance.

We started off with a carriage full of gaiety and anticipation. I looped my arm through Jake's as he drove his spanking pair of mares. I looked around at Andrew who had his arm carelessly flung over Phoebe's shoulder. I smiled at him and he nodded.

We entered the new Masonic hall where the dance music already filled the big room. Two fiddles, a banjo, a guitar and piano provided the dance music. Excitement bounced around the walls as dancers twirled their partners around and around.

Dancing with Jake was a dream come true. We seemed fashioned for each other and he held me close as he gracefully danced through the other celebrants. With a feeling of near euphoria, I followed his lead.

Jake went over to speak to his fellow firemen and Dr. Blake came up to me asking me for a dance. I reluctantly agreed. As we danced, he kept up a patter as if to entertain me but all I could think of was Jake who filled me with love and anticipation.

I realized the doctor had asked a question. "What did you say, doctor?" I asked.

"I asked if you'd reconsider my proposal. I think we'd make a delightful team in Olympia. I could do a lot for you."

I stepped out of his embrace and said, "Doctor, I appreciate your feelings for me but I'm in love with Jake and I'm going to marry him." The moment of decision had arrived without me consciously debating it.

After leaving the doctor in the middle of the floor, I went to Jake and pulled him from his friends. "I will marry you as soon as the cabin is finished, my dear." Dr. Blake's repeated proposals prompted my action. It was time to make the final commitment to my love. Jake hugged me, kissed me and we laughed with his friends who surrounded us.

Zona and Walt made a lovely, sedate couple among the younger crowd and I marveled at how well my brother danced. I tripped the light fantastic with him a couple of times but the other dances he had with Phoebe. It appeared she was as taken with him as he was with her.

The firemen, one by one, danced with me and I realized what a brotherhood these fellows shared with Jake. Finally he took my hand, pulled me from my last partner and said, "Sorry, guys, she's my girl and you'll have to find other partners for the rest of the dance. Her dance card is full, of me." He looked down at me and smiled that darn quirky smile.

"I am full of you, Jake, be it rake or blunderbuss. I love you very much and can't wait for the cabin to be finished," I told him, my eyes speaking as loud as my voice.

"It looks as if we really made some bucks for the new town hall. It will be great to have a place for our Columbia fire engine and a place to meet. Olympia is growing up," Jake said.

"I'm so pleased to be part of a community that's building rather than living in the south that's so devastated. It's exciting to look toward the future instead of the past," I said as I glided in Jake's arms.

"I'm excited about the future, too, sweetheart, with you always near my heart. I've never felt like this about any woman I've ever met," he said solemnly.

"I can echo that, my dear. This feeling I have for you is brand new. Hurry up with that cabin," I said as I hugged him tighter.

I noticed that Zona whispered to the piano player and he nodded with a sly smile on his face. He spoke to the other musicians and soon their faces were wreathed in grins. With a downbeat, a lively tune picked up the pace and Zona hiked her skirts up nearly to her knees as she kicked and strutted in a fancy cake-walk. All the other dancers gave way and she performed in center stage.

The look on Walt's face was one of disbelief. I couldn't determine if he experienced shock or wonderment about this woman in his life. Zona finished her dance to a great round of applause and laughter. She wiped her brow with the hanky she always kept in her sleeve and gave me a huge, smug smile as if to say, "There, I showed them."

She came to me and put her arms around me and asked, "Now what do you think of Zona? I haven't done that in a long time. I guess it's about time I showed the person I really am." I hugged her laughing too hard to answer her question.

"You're speechless, honey. In case you didn't realize it, I've done a lot of things in my life including the dance you just saw, singing in a saloon, promoting drinks but one thing I never did was sell my body. I came close but I was never hungry enough." She smiled and hugged me again. "I've never really had a woman friend," she said, gave me another hug and added, "Until now."

As the music continued, Jake and I were so wrapped up in each other we failed to see others looking askance at the figure in the doorway. The feeling of concern finally made itself felt and we, too, looked at the wraith of a man with a crutch lodged in his armpit. His clothes were ragged and his emaciated form told of illness and pain.

All of a sudden, I knew who he was. I called, "John" then blackness descended.

Ascending out of the void, I felt a cold cloth on my forehead. I slowly opened my eyes and they focused on familiar faces around me, Zona, Jake, Andrew, Phoebe, and John Jewell, my husband. I struggled to a sitting position supported by Jake.

The shock of seeing John after all these years had knocked me senseless. "Everyone, I'd like you to meet my husband, John Jewell," I said. I know I should have exhibited some sort of warmness and welcome but those feelings were beyond me. The pain I saw on Jake's face mirrored what I felt. A few minutes ago my life was filled with rose petals and now they had turned to ashes.

John nodded to those assembled and they nodded back in this very awkward confrontation. I tried to ease the atmosphere. "I think John and I need to talk," I said. "I know you all care about me but I think my husband and I need to be alone for a bit to straighten things out."

Jake glared at John, kissed me on the cheek in defiance, and left with the others. The muted sound of music came through the anteroom door as John and I sat and looked at each other.

His southern baritone voice, weakened now, said, "It took me a long time to find you, Hannah," he said. "I went back to Ruby Acres and saw that it was gone. I found Pearl's gravestone but none of my sisters or brother. Do you know what happened?"

"When we heard the Yankees were a day away, they all snatched what they could and left. As for Pearl, I tried to keep her alive but we had nothing, not even decent food and she wasted away." Now tears coursed down my cheeks, not for John, but for my precious little girl.

"What about you, John? I tried to find out what happened to you from both the Confederate officials and finally from the Union Army. They told me there had been an outbreak of typhoid fever in the camp where you were listed with injuries. He couldn't tell me if you had survived."

"I had a bad leg, still do," he said, patting his knee. "I also got typhoid but survived somehow. A lot of men died. I don't remember much after that except I knew I had to get back to Ruby Acres and find my family. I stumped around with my crutch and found nothing, not even you," he added with a hint of accusation.

"There was no way I could stay on the plantation," I said in my defense. "We had very little food, Ruby Acres had been devastated, and I lived in a slave cabin with Lucy, the only darky that stayed with me. I tried to keep the plantation together so you'd have something to come home to but I failed. If you blame me for that, so be it."

"It was a real disappointment for me to see that there was nothing left there, not even my wife," John said still with an accusing glint in his eye.

Had I ever loved this man?

"I felt I had no other choice, John. When my brother wrote and told me he needed me to care for his little girl after his wife's death, I could see no other way to survive. He sent me the money to make the trip and I've been here ever since. I did leave my name and address with the Union authorities."

"That's how I found you," John replied. "I went to find out if one of my friends was listed as a survivor. I told him my name, too, and he said he had a note for me. At least you provided a way for me to find you, Hannah."

"And here you are, John. We'll have to make some different arrangements than those we had planned," I said, thinking about the love of my life waiting on the other side of the door to the anteroom.

Chapter Twenty Three

Yes, indeed, other arrangements had to be made. The enormity of the implications surrounding John's return came down on me like a ton of bricks. "Patience, Hannah," I told myself, "One step at a time." First the decision about the rest of the night had to be made. I turned to John who sat on a bench in the anteroom with his leg outstretched.

"Where are you staying in Olympia?" I asked.

"At the Pacific House," he replied. "My leg hurts so badly. Is there a doctor in town?"

"Yes, in fact he's here at the dance. I'll go find him and then I have to talk to a few people." I mentally pulled myself up by my bootstraps and went into the big hall. I saw Jake, who looked at me with a question in his eyes. How I loved that man.

I found Doctor Blake and took him in to see John while I searched for Andrew. He and Phoebe came toward me along with Jake and Zona. "You're all concerned in the decisions I have to make," I began with a deep sigh. "I want you all to know that the man in there is not the man I married but I have an obligation to take care of him. Andrew, can he live with us on the homestead for a while?"

"Sure, Hannah, if that's what you want," Andrew replied as he looked at Phoebe. The two seemed to have a tacit understanding.

"It's not what I want but what I must do. Tonight, if you and Jake will help me, we'll take him back to his room at the Pacific House then go out to the homestead in the morning. Abby's old enough now to climb the ladder into the loft and I'll sleep on her pallet in the bedroom. John can have the bed." Those around me nodded in reluctant agreement.

"Jake, can we take a walk outside?"

He ducked his head in agreement, got my wrap, and we went out into the cool, midnight air. I turned to him, put my arms around his neck and he held me tightly as if he never wanted to let me go. "I love you with all my heart, dear Jake, and will until the day I die," I began as I felt the tears running down my cheeks. "But I have never shirked my duty and I can't begin now. It's who I am. As far as I'm concerned, John and I are linked legally but that's the only way. I have to take care of him."

Jake hugged me tighter, took a deep breath and said, "God knows I understand but I don't have to like it, sweetheart. I was so happy tonight when you said you'd marry me when I finished the cabin. It will be very empty for me since the one I built it for won't be in it." He swallowed as if he had a lump in his throat.

"I want you to know I release you from your promise to marry me. I don't want you to wait for me, Jake; you have to get on with your life."

"I will wait for you, Hannah; you're the only woman I want. Could we see each other now and then, just to talk?" Jake asked.

I nodded and said, "You bet, my love, and maybe you could hold me and kiss me just a little."

He held me closer and kissed me passionately. That would have to do for now. We went back into the ballroom and I headed toward the anteroom where my bleak future awaited me.

Doctor Blake explained he had given John a little laudanum for his pain. He said, "I guess you won't be marrying Jake now, since your husband has come back." The smirk earned my glare.

With the help of my friends we got John to his lodgings placing his crutch next to his bed. He drowsed as I told him, "We'll be back to get you in the morning and take you to the homestead, John. My brother has approved of my plan and I hope you appreciate what he's doing for us."

"I heard the doctor say something about you marrying again. You can't, you're my wife." He drifted off to sleep with those words on his lips.

I wept into my pillow that night knowing that my glorious future with Jake lay in shambles. How could I stand it, to take care of one man while I loved another? I prayed for strength.

The next morning after a fitful night at Phoebe's we readied ourselves for the trip out of town. I told them I wanted to walk down and talk to Zona first. They agreed to pick me up at the Gold Bar.

As I went into the restaurant's parlor it seemed Zona waited for me. She enfolded me in her arms and held me quietly as I cried. "How can I bear this, Zona?" I cried. "I love Jake so much and now I can't marry him."

"You're stronger than you think, honey. You'll do what your mind and heart tell you to do." She patted my head.

"But my head and heart don't agree," I replied. "My head tells me I have a duty to John because of the marriage contract but my heart tells me Jake is the love of my life." I sobbed as Zona held me.

"Honey, you know both in your head and heart you have to take care of John. You couldn't be happy unless you fulfilled what you see as your obligation. Things will work out for you. Listen to Zona, she knows," she said with a final pat. "Now, wipe your eyes, and get ready to meet your responsibilities. You know I'm here for you when things get too tough."

I pulled back, wiped my face and hugged her. "Thank you, my dear friend, for being such a rock for me."

The gaiety of the night before did not accompany us to the homestead. All of us remained silent and I wondered what each of them thought. Andrew probably deplored the fact that his alliance with Phoebe wouldn't happen any time soon; Jake no doubt cursed his luck that John had appeared just as we had promised ourselves to each other; what John might think didn't enter into the equation.

As we pulled up in the cabin's dooryard, John said, "It's small, isn't it. Not much like Ruby Acres."

"No, it's not like Ruby Acres, and I appreciate that fact every day," I said with little patience.

Andrew glanced at John and said, "You don't have to stay if you don't want to. It's up to you."

"I have no other place to go, Andrew, and my wife lives here. I'll stay," he said peevishly.

The animosity between the two men set the tone for the days that followed. John constantly complained while Andrew glowered. I realized that John's leg probably caused some pain but I felt he blew it all out of proportion.

At first, he protested about the fact I didn't share his bed. "John, we're husband and wife in name only," I told him. "I'm in love with another man and he's in love with me. I am taking care of you out of my obligation as your wife, but not for any other reason."

"I plan to live a very long time, Hannah, and I expect you to take care of me so you can forget about your boyfriend. Now, I need some more laudanum for this dratted pain."

Chapter Twenty Four

The only joys during those dreary winter days were the visits Jake made to the homestead. He and Andrew usually stayed outside talking about crops, town events, and I suppose about the situation in which we all found ourselves.

Doctor Blake came regularly and ministered to John, plying him with laudanum. I expressed my objection but he and John took the decision away from me.

"John, can't you see Doctor Blake is overdosing you with that drug?" I asked in exasperation. "It's addictive and the doctor feels powerful when one of his patients can't do without it."

"My leg hurts so badly, Hannah, I can hardly stand it," he whined. I wondered what had happened to his southern baritone voice.

"It might get better if you got out of that bed and moved to strengthen your leg," I said knowing he would not follow my advice. He only got up for meals and trips to the privy. I refused to serve his meals in bed or to empty a slop bucket.

"You know I can't walk much," he said. "I do the best I can. I'm not strong like you. Maybe that's why I married you, because you seemed strong," he said with a speculative look at me.

"I've wondered why you courted me. I'm plain so I know it wasn't for my looks. I thought I was in love with you but now I know that it was more appreciation than love."

"I thought Ruby Acres needed a person like you. It needed someone strong to take care of things."

"You had slaves for that, John."

"Not someone to take charge, someone from the family."

"You're certainly right there. Anyhow, that was a different life. It's gone and now we have to cope with what there is now. Don't count on any affection from me. I don't expect anything from you, either, but the least you could do is appreciate what Andrew has provided for you since you have nothing."

"Oh, I have something, Hannah, I have you and don't you forget it."

One spring day, Jake rode his beautiful mare into the dooryard. I saw him look at me through the window. I went out even though John called out to me. I ignored his whine. Jake took my hand and we walked along the stream that threatened to go over its banks after the heavy rain that had deluged us.

"It's like I don't exist unless I'm with you," he said as he turned me around and kissed me ardently.

"I feel the same, Jake, my love. I can hardly stand the life I live now. The only saving grace is your visit now and again." I kissed him again. "Jake, is there any free land around your homestead?"

"I think so," he said. "There is a lot of free land to the north of me. Why do you want to know?"

"A married woman can claim up to 320 acres according to the Donation Land Claim Law, if I read it right in the *Evening Olympian*. Could you find out about that for me? There's no need to tell anyone else. It'll be our secret." I said.

"Now that I can do and that's a positive step toward our future." He grabbed me, kissed me and held me tightly.

"Please take your hands off my wife," John said with accusation in his voice.

Jake slowly pulled my arms from around his neck, held my hands and glared at John. He said, looking at me, "I'll do what you ask, sweetheart."

"What did you ask him to do, Hannah?" John asked petulantly.

Jake answered for me, "That is none of your damn business, sir."

"She's my wife and that makes it my business," John replied.

This time I answered, "Wife in name only, John, and you'd better accept it."

After giving me a final hand squeeze, Jake strode through the woods toward the dooryard. John and I followed slowly.

"I thought your leg hurt so bad you couldn't walk, John. Have you had a miraculous recovery?" I asked just short of a sneer.

"It's hurting really bad now, Hannah. If you had come when I called I wouldn't have followed you. Could you help me back?" he whined.

I sighed, shrugged, and put his arm around my shoulder to help him back to the cabin. It seemed a torturous trip that took hours but actually we reached the cabin in fifteen minutes.

I helped him into bed, covered him and started from the room. He stopped me with his usual plaint. "I need some laudanum, Hannah. I can hardly stand the pain."

"Don't you believe me when I say you're an addict?" I asked in exasperation. "The more you have, the more you want. You need to wean yourself away from it."

"Please, Hannah, I need it badly right now after all that walking," he wailed.

"All right, John, it's on your own head." I went to the cupboard, reached down the laudanum bottle and found it almost empty. With a feeling of desolation, I realized he'd been dosing himself between his calls to me for the drug.

Andrew returned from his trip to town for more seed to plant after he had tilled the soil. As he came into the cabin with the supplies I'd ordered, he said, "I invited Jake and Jason for Sunday dinner. Jason has a puppy he wants Abby to see." He looked at me as if he wondered what my reaction might be.

"That sounds good to me. Abby has had a dismal existence since John came. I still teach her but her exuberance disappeared after I worked so hard for her sunny disposition. It's as if she walks around in fear," I said.

"I think you're right. Let's not leave her in the house alone with John. Is that okay with you?" he asked.

"I agree completely, Andrew. Under the influence of that drug, who knows what might happen." I paused and continued, "I don't know how to thank you for all you've done for me. You rescued me from the south and now in this horrible situation with John. I've tried to think of how we can solve this problem but nothing comes to mind. Maybe I could get a job in town and take him there."

"We'll survive this together, Hannah. You saved my bacon when you came to take care of Abby." He smiled and added, "And take care of me, too. You've added a lot to our lives and I appreciate it."

We hugged each other awkwardly and turned to our own tasks. My spirit seemed lighter after our talk and I knew I wasn't alone. I mentally planned Sunday dinner as I went about my chores. The thought of Jake and his son here in this cabin gave me something to look forward to.

Chapter Twenty Five

The long-awaited Sunday dawned clear and sparkling. I wondered if my spirit painted the sky so gloriously or if it truly reflected nature's bounty. As I worked around the cabin, I thought about the planting we had done during the week with Abby happy again to be tilling her own garden. Andrew and I made sure she never spent time alone in the cabin with John.

I thought John's condition deteriorated but nothing I said convinced him to wean himself away from that awful drug. Doctor Blake had been out during the week bringing a brand new bottle of it. I hated it with a passion and after I explained why to Andrew in reference to his wife, he agreed with me. Every time John whined for a dose, a look of disgust passed over my brother's face.

Abby's anticipation echoed mine. She hadn't seen her friend for a long time and I could tell excitement filled her. She helped me with the household chores and hustled up the ladder to the loft to get her latest books her father had brought from town at my request.

"I'm going to teach Jason some more reading," she said proudly. "I can hardly wait to show him my new books." She was alive with enthusiasm. I felt thankful for the temporary change.

Soon we heard the wagon pull into the dooryard and besides his son, Jake had brought Phoebe. The light in Andrew's eyes filled my heart. My brother swung his sweetheart down from the wagon while Jake lifted his son down along with a black puppy whose large paws told of how big he would be at maturity.

Abby ran out and begged to hold the dog. Jason relaxed his hold and the girl hugged the puppy with rapture on her face.

"I have something just for you, Abby," Jake said as he reached once again into the wagon's bed. He lifted out a small quilt and handed it to Abby. She looked at him, puzzled about his gift. Then the quilt wiggled and out came the head of a beautiful kitten.

"This is just for me?" she asked with tears sprouting from her eyes.

"Yes, sweetheart, just for you. You have to name her, though, because she needs to know in case you call to her." He looked at me over Abby's head and we spoke volumes with our eyes.

Abby carefully unwrapped the kitten. "I'll call her Tiny Tilly like that girl in the book you read to me," she said to me as she petted the newly-named cat. "Can I get her some milk, Aunt Hannah?" she asked.

I took her into the cabin and we found a dish, poured some milk into it and Tiny Tilly lost no time in slurping up the first meal in her new home.

With dinner on the table, I called to John that we ready to eat. I heard a moan and then a shuffle as he roused himself from his bed. He hobbled into the front room where the rest of us already lined the table. He nodded to the group, assumed his seat and then the rest of us ignored him as we chatted about mutual concerns.

Jake cleared his throat, and said, "I got the papers for you, Hannah, just as you asked. John has to sign them, too."

"What papers are those, Hannah? What are you planning now?" John asked plaintively.

"A married woman can get up to 320 acres of free land under the Donation Land Claim Law and I thought we should have a place of our own so Andrew can get on with his life. It sounded like a good idea for us," I answered calmly.

"Why didn't you consult me, Hannah, you are my wife?" John asked in his usual supercilious way.

"I didn't want to bother you with details until I knew for sure we could do it. Jake has someone who will build us a cabin so we'll be on our own," I said with a nonchalance I really didn't feel.

"Okay, I'll sign the papers but the rest is up to you. I'm too ill to help physically. Of course, I could oversee the project with my experience on Ruby Acres," he said with disdain.

"Fine, we'll do the paper work after some apple pie. Everyone ready for dessert?" I asked with a wide smile that covered my inner thoughts and planning.

Abby and I cleared the table following the meal while Jason played with his new puppy. Tiny Tilly had curled up on the hearth and slept peacefully. As John limped toward the bedroom, the puppy nipped at his heel. Balancing on his crutch, he kicked out at the animal and it yelped in pain and terror.

Jason gathered the pup to his chest and glared at John, "Don't you ever hurt my dog again, you old man," he asserted. Oh, my, I thought, another confrontation. I wondered if there would ever be peace in my domain.

After the land acquisition became a fact, John wanted to go see our property. Andrew harnessed the horse and we got John into the wagon bed settled on some quilts. He said he was too ill to ride on the seat. Andrew and Abby settled on the seat beside me and my brother drove us smartly out of the dooryard.

It had been so long since I had been away that I thoroughly enjoyed the trip down into Olympia and out past Priest's Point to the land north of Jake's spread. I could barely see the cabin he had built through the trees. He had planted a stake at the far end of his property and I knew that beyond it lay the land I had claimed.

I pointed out the beginning of the property to John and Andrew as we slowly drove by. We stopped along the narrow road to gaze at lush surroundings that might hold the answer to our dilemma. Andrew helped John out of the wagon and we slowly walked through the trees and meadows to pick a spot for the cabin.

John complained about his leg continually but wanted to choose the cabin site himself so the rest of us endured. He decided on a large meadow surrounded by tall evergreen trees. I don't know if his choice reflected his judicial powers or if his leg would not take any more walking but I agreed it seemed a good spot for a cabin.

Andrew pounded a stake into the ground to mark the place and said he'd tell Jake where to have a cabin started. I hoped it could be finished soon to give my brother a chance at a new life with Phoebe. He deserved it. What my life would be like with John in the cabin remained to be seen. At least I would be close to Jake. That thought brightened my day.

Chapter Twenty Six

The thought of my own land filled me with a quiet peace. For some reason I didn't see John as that land's owner. The free acres didn't mean the cabin could be built for nothing. Jake had arranged for Ernie Ellis, the logger who accompanied us on the fire engine odyssey from New York to Olympia, to help with its construction in return for the surrounding trees. Ernie came out to see me so we could plan the cabin's layout.

"I want a two-room cabin with a loft, Ernie," I told him. I found that sometimes a curtain just didn't define a bedroom.

The roly-poly logger started sketching and talking at the same time. He was as voluble as ever. I pointed out things I wanted while he drew the plan leaning over the table.

"We could put windows on two sides of the cabin with a full-length porch across the front. A door both back and front would work really well." His excitement reflected mine as we talked.

John hobbled in with his crutch. He seldom left his bed but he must have heard our voices and what we planned. "This is Ernie Ellis, John. He's going to build our cabin in exchange for the logging rights on my land."

He nodded coolly and said, "This land is ours, Hannah, not just yours, and I think I should be consulted about the cabin. We really need at least three rooms with big windows on each side. A gracious porch should surround it like a veranda. Those were popular in the south."

"John, we're not in the south now. We're in Washington Territory on the west coast. Customs are different here, and house plans have to be adapted to the land. Ernie here knows how to go about that, don't you Ernie?" I asked as I turned to him.

"I sure do, Hannah, I helped Jake with his cabin and built one for myself. It ain't so hard but we have to agree early on just what you want."

"So Jake recommended you, did he? I wish he'd keep his nose out of my business," John said testily.

"I know Ernie from our trip together from New York. He's a good logger and a good builder. He helped Andrew with his cabin, too. I feel fully confident in his ability and if you don't have an alternative, he will build our cabin to my specifications since I seem to be the most practical one of this family." I turned away from John and ignored him just as did Ernie. He finally went back to bed glowering. He seemed to have enough energy to exert himself when he felt slighted but for little else.

Andrew came in while we continued to bat ideas around for the cabin. He looked at what Ernie had drawn, nodded, and said, "It looks like you've covered every need. What about out-buildings?"

"The cabin first, then the outbuildings," Ernie said. "We'll need to know what kind of livestock Hannah will have before we can build them." His exuberance infected both Andrew and me.

I knew that Ernie had to fell some of the trees around the clearing before he could start the cabin and through the summer I made several trips to my land and occasionally Jake would meet me there where we could talk without John around.

"I've got some fire department news, sweetheart. You know we've been agitating for a fire hall and that dance we held brought in some good money even though it ended badly for us. The town borrowed $500 to buy a site and bought one on Fourth Street between Washington and Franklin. Now all we have to do is raise the rest of the money. Town offices and the fire department will share the quarters. The Columbia fire engine will finally have a good home."

"Olympia's really growing up, Jake, and I like feeling I'm a part of it. This is such a contrast to the old south where everything reached its peak and is in decline while out here, it's upward and onward. This place is filled with free spirits, and you're one of them my dear Jake."

He pulled me to him and said, "And so are you, sweetheart. You're a strong, dedicated person, just the right kind of woman for me."

"What if I'm too strong, Jake, and not feminine enough?" I asked.

"It's all part of the package I love, sweetheart." He kissed me passionately and I responded just as ardently.

"I'll like having you close even though you won't be in our cabin," he said pensively. "I hate the thought of you caring for that crippled bigot but you have to do what you think is right." He kissed me again.

"I've named my place, Jake. I expect John will throw a fit but I don't care. This land is now Jade Meadows. Isn't that a lovely name?"

"Yep, it is and just as beautiful and elegant as its mistress," he replied.

Occasionally, John would insist on going with me to my land. He might protest it was *our* land but I knew within my soul that it was mine. When I told him what I had named the homestead, he reacted predictably.

"It should be Ruby Acres Two," he said. "My plantation has always been Ruby Acres and this land should be named the same although I realize we have to add that it's number two."

"Say what you like, John, but this is not a plantation as I've explained so many times before. It's homestead land in my name and it is called Jade Meadows." Sometimes my patience ran so thin I thought it would break.

After the last visit when John went with me, he needed help from Andrew and me to get him to bed. He seemed to be going downhill and I railed inwardly about his use of laudanum. I should let it go and just let him overdose himself into oblivion but I couldn't live with that. It went against my nature to consciously contribute to another's demise.

With John ensconced in bed most of the time, Abby's nature began to blossom again and Tiny Tilly was a godsend for her. The kitten joined in our lessons and seemed to absorb them although I knew it was the curiosity that infected most felines.

Andrew's homestead broadened as he cut trees and tilled the land. The garden prospered through the summer and the harvest was good. He slaughtered a pig so we'd have cured ham through the winter and he even shot two beautiful brown-eyed deer whose eyes haunted me. The venison would taste good and enhance our larder but I had to turn away from their hanging bodies.

As fall painted the northwest tapestry with gold and red punctuated by the green of the fir trees, Ernie had felled enough trees so that he could commence with the cabin. Jake had found some lumber to go along with the logs for the foundation. On every visit, I took rocks from the streambed for the fireplace.

Joy filled me as I saw the foundation take form and impatience for its completion joined the joy. It felt so right to do this, settle onto my own Jade Meadows in spite of John's attitude. It would be so much better to be on our own without inflicting his sour temper on my brother and his little girl. I knew Andrew grew anxious to have his own family including Phoebe alone on his homestead.

Life would not be easy here, but it would be my life on my land.

Chapter Twenty Seven

The territory's winter came in with a blast of cold, drenching rain that turned into snow to usher in 1868. The construction of my cabin on Jade Meadows became the only hope for my new year. John continued to deteriorate and I hoped we could move into the cabin before he worsened.

Phoebe had offered some of the excess furniture from her boarding house to help us set up housekeeping. Andrew donated a ham and some chickens along with anything I wanted that the garden had produced and I had canned.

The time came in early spring when we thought the time was right for the move. John had chosen not to visit the cabin for a few months but I think he looked forward to moving, too. With a wagon full of supplies, we put John on top of the bedding Andrew had given us and my brother drove. Abby sat on the seat between us. She had been to my homestead and liked gamboling in the long grass.

After we arrived and jumped down from the wagon, we both tried to rouse John but he was lethargic. It took just a moment for me to make one of the beds and we practically carried him into the cabin and laid him down. I started a fire in the fireplace to take the chill from the cabin.

As I began to make order out of chaos, I already felt a calmness descend on me. I had a home of my own and I knew that Andrew could now pursue his own life. He had a future with Phoebe and his excitement at the prospect made me feel the time had been right for me to leave his household. Abby would be taken care of and so would Andrew. I wondered how Phoebe would feel to become a homesteader instead of a landlady. She hadn't decided yet whether to lease the boarding house or sell it.

I heard a horse ride down the lane and stop outside my door. Ernie jumped down from his horse and I met him at the door with a big hug for this pudgy guy who had built my cabin.

"Oh, Ernie, you've done so much for me; a cabin, a privy, a chicken coop, and even a hitching rail. I can only repay you with a meal now and then. Maybe I'll start tutoring or sewing or cooking to earn some money," I bubbled. And this tall, plain woman seldom bubbled.

"Don't worry about it, Hannah. The trees I felled more than paid me for my labor. Jake furnished most of the lumber," he added as an afterthought.

"Come in and have a cup of coffee. I have to learn how to cook over an open fire again but that's not hard to do. It just limits what I can fix to eat," I said, pulling him into the cabin.

"Can't say I'd turn down a cup of coffee," he said as he doffed his hat and joined me in front of the fire.

"You did such a good job on the fireplace. It draws well and adds very little smoke to the room," I rambled. "And there's so much storage in the loft. I'll be filling it as I sort things out."

"I can help, if you want," Ernie said. "Just let me know." It seemed the voluble Ernie had changed places with me. Having a human to talk to with whom I had no emotional link helped settle me down.

We chatted, drank coffee and made more plans for Jade Meadows. How wonderful it was to look forward instead of being mired in the grave issues that faced me.

John called from the bedroom, "Hannah, my leg hurts. Get me some medicine," he ordered feebly.

My duties burdened me again but the respite buoyed me.

The chore of storing all of our goods was an exercise that I thoroughly enjoyed, again because this was mine. I refused to consider that any of it belonged to John. He was my patient but he had no part in the exercise to make this my space.

It was simple to make a pot of soup that would last several days and that was about the only food John could eat. I fed him in bed now and he arose only to make the trek to the privy. I faced the fact that soon I would have to empty a slop jar for him. He had energy enough to demand laudanum, though.

The rattle of a wagon awoke me one spring morning. I rushed to dress and pull back my hair into a hasty bun before I looked out the window. Jake and Ernie let down the tailgate of the wagon to unload a small cook stove. I stood in the doorway with my mouth hanging open. This was an answer to another prayer. I wondered how many prayer answers I had left.

"Is that for me?" I asked foolishly.

"Of course, sweetheart. Zona had this stove she didn't use and wanted me to bring it to you." He put his arms around me and kissed me while Ernie looked on with approval.

The two men grunted and pulled and pushed to get the iron stove into the cabin and set it up along the far wall. "I don't know how to thank you again, Ernie, and you Jake. Please tell Zona she saved my life once more," I said fervently. This would simplify my life and ease my burden. I could now cook meals instead of just soup and coffee.

"I'll fix Sunday dinner for you two angels," I said. "How's that for payment?" They both nodded and I had something special to look forward to.

Delicious smells of baked ham filled the cabin on Sunday and I anticipated the company of my two angels. Thank goodness Phoebe had given me enough chairs to fit around the table and I had brought my special rocker that Andrew had given me.

John felt my joy and asked why I was so happy. "We're having guests for dinner," I told him. "Ernie and Jake are coming. I had to find a way to thank them for bringing me the stove."

"Well, I guess I could come out and eat with you all. After all, I'm the head of this household," he said with a bit more spirit than he had shown for weeks. I hoped he'd drowse through the time my two friends were here.

Thinking of the friends produced them. My heart did its usual flip when I saw the tall Texan with the black hat pulled down over his brow. He swung down from his horse with great grace while Ernie clambered down from his mount.

Jake hugged me and kissed me on the cheek. I wondered what John would have done if he'd had enough energy to get out of bed.

We chatted before the fireplace about the doings in Olympia. Ernie had returned to his voluble self and his words spilled out. "The town hall is well underway and we're talking about another loan to finish the building. The town council will meet upstairs and the Columbia will finally have a suitable home," he chattered. "The guys can hardly wait for it to be ready. We've used the engine a few times already with great results. There was that fire up Fourth Street that we got to early and saved the building. Sure gives us a good feeling. It's really amazing what you can do with proper equipment." He finally ran out of breath.

"Well, gentlemen, I think the feast can be put on the table now. I'll wake John so he can join us," I said. A look of disappointment crossed Jake's face. I had to call John and I liked it less than Jake.

I went into the bedroom and John dozed so I let him sleep while the three of us enjoyed dinner together with lots of lively conversation and remembrances of our trip around the Horn.

After we settled before the fire, well fed and comfortable, I went into the bedroom again and tried to waken John. He seemed comatose. I rushed into the other room and asked one of them to go for Doctor Blake as fast as he could. Ernie rushed out while Jake joined me in the bedroom. He, too, tried to rouse my husband. This was something I was not equipped to handle by myself no matter my reservations about the good doctor.

When I heard the rattle of the trap, I ran to the window. Dr. Blake hitched his horse, grabbed his bag and I met him at the door.

"What's the hurry, Hannah?" he asked.

"John's not responding to my words or touch. He's not even complaining about how bad his leg hurts. You need to help him, Doctor Blake," I urged.

I ushered him into the bedroom of my cabin while Jake stood by the fireplace. What catastrophe awaited me now, I thought as I wrung my hands in frustration.

Chapter Twenty Eight

Jake helped Dr. Blake put John in the doctor's trap and we made a mad dash to Olympia. Priest's Point flashed by and all I could think of was what if John died or what if he didn't. I knew it would happen eventually but I couldn't contemplate either scenario. All I knew was we had to get to town. Jake rode alongside us and looked at me occasionally with compassion on his face.

The doctor explained about his dispensary in the back of his office as we flew along. "That's one reason I wanted you to marry me, Hannah, to help with it. I have a couple of hospital beds and some equipment. I'll be able to care for John better there than in your cabin." He lashed the horse again as we rolled into town pulling up with a flourish in front of his office. Jake hitched both horses and then helped Doctor Blake lift John down from the wagon bed.

I huddled on a chair in the dispensary while the two men undressed John so the doctor could do his job. Jake said, "I'll be at the Gold Bar, Hannah, in case you need me." He touched my shoulder and left.

I watched with morbid fascination while the doctor searched John's body. I saw the crooked leg that had caused so much pain. The scars frightened me and told of massive damage to the limb. John had always concealed the sight from me.

I felt a warm arm around my shoulder and looked up into Zona's compassionate face. She always knew when I needed her. No one could have a better friend. I could no longer sit still so I stood next to Zona and we watched the procedure.

Doctor Blake seemed to do a thorough examination then suddenly he grabbed his ear trumpet and placed it on John's chest. He felt his pulse, looked into his eye as he pulled up the lid, and shook his head.

"I'm sorry, Hannah, he's gone. His heart just gave out." He and I looked at one another and he knew what I thought. I could have accused him of overdosing on laudanum. I could have threatened to have his license revoked. I could have shouted the truth to the world but I just felt drained. I no longer felt like tilting at windmills.

I dropped into the chair and sobbed. My reaction might have been from relief but the feeling went deeper. It brought back all of the grief from those war years; the losses, the deprivation, my daughter's death and the devastation of the south.

Zona pulled me up and hugged me tightly as if to give me strength. "How can I be widowed twice and married only once?" I hiccupped.

"Life's not always fair, honey. I had the feeling you didn't love John, that it was a marriage in name only."

"You're right, my friend, I didn't love him now but we did have a pretty good life together before the war. It seems it's just such a waste. The war and his pain turned him into a different man." I wiped my eyes and wondered what I had to do next.

"Don't you worry about the arrangements," Zona said. "I'll see that everything is taken care of. Now you go over to the Gold Bar and Lucy will watch out for you." She patted my shoulder, offered a handkerchief to dry my eyes and I obeyed her as most people did.

In the Gold Bar parlor I found Lucy, told her what had happened, and she indeed took care of me plying me with hot tea and a neck rub. Jake came into the parlor and we looked solemnly at one another. God only knew what the future held for us but all I felt now was grief and loss inexplicable as it might be. He nodded and left the room.

Zona had arranged everything; the coffin, the burial, and the minister. The small cortege headed south on Olympia's Main Street toward the cemetery with a cold rain matching the solemnity of the occasion. I moved like an automaton, going where I was led, doing what I was told, and taking little notice of the few people around me.

I couldn't think beyond the next minute. My mind felt numbed. Lethargy filled me and I just let Zona lead me back into her parlor. "Honey, I want you to stay with me a few days until you adjust to this new wrinkle in your life. It takes time, I know. Just listen to Zona; she's been more emotional places than you could ever dream of."

I nodded looking at the black dress she had loaned me. One thing I knew, I would not wear mourning. Times had changed and I was no longer bound by southern tradition. I began to peel the gown off. "I want to wear my own clothes now, Zona. I have to reinvent myself into the kind of person I want to be without considering anyone else," I said with the first moment of lucidity.

"What about Jake, Hannah?" Zona asked, never one to shy away from the tough questions.

"I'll have to figure that out, too. I need time by myself to sort out my feelings, my future and how to cope with the present," I said. Determination began to fill me as I said those words. Of course I could figure it all out. I would go back to my Jade Meadows and consider all of the options for my future.

Jake drove me home, what a wonderful word that was. He swung me down from the wagon, looked intently into my eyes and asked, "What about us, sweetheart?"

"Dear Jake, I need some time to sort this entire situation out. I'm sure we have a future together but right now I'm dealing with emotions in relation to John's death that I didn't expect. I feel guilty about not doing more to help him." I said quietly.

"You feel guilty?" he erupted. "You did everything you could for that man including warning him repeatedly about his use of drugs. You cared for his needs, absorbed his abuse, and fixed a place for him in your cabin."

"Maybe I feel guilty because he should have had my love and didn't. I cared for him as another human being, not my husband," I said in measured tones.

"You know that's hogwash. He certainly didn't treat you as a treasured wife." He strode to the wagon and drove out of the yard. I wondered if he'd ever return.

I really felt no grief any more and began to revel in my own domain. I had never had a place of my own before nor had I really been independent and thoroughly enjoyed the feeling. I no longer had to ask anyone's permission to move furniture, hang a picture or two, decide what to store in the loft and at night I could sleep in a bedroom devoid of anyone but me. I'd look around me and say to myself, "This all belongs to me."

As I tidied around my cabin, I thought about how to support myself. I had training as a librarian and I had taught at least two people to read. I decided I needed to know if the grade school in Olympia could use a tutor or reading teacher, or maybe even a librarian.

Although I hadn't seen Jake since he stormed off the day he brought me back to Jade Meadows, he was my nearest neighbor. I hated to ask him for help but had no other choice. My feelings about him were ambivalent even though the thought of his crooked smile and smoky blue eyes could jolt my heart.

The warm spring day enfolded me as I walked through the woods to Jake's cabin. There seemed to be no one around and, disappointed, I left a note for him to come see me and what I wanted. Now all I could do was wait.

Chapter Twenty Nine

Two days passed. I dusted, I swept, remade my bed a dozen times, cleaned the dooryard and still I saw no sign of Jake. Disconsolate, I decided I'd have to walk to town if I wanted to find a job at the school. I had never seen the school but I remember Jake telling me about it.

On the third evening when I had determined I would walk to town the next day, Jake rode in on his beautiful bay mare. I went out to greet him, so glad he had come in response to my summons.

He swung down from his horse and stood looking at me. "So you want a ride to town to look for a job?" he asked with little emotion. How I wished he would hold me in his arms again but maybe neither of us was ready to heal the breach.

"Yes, Jake, I would. Do you think the grade school would hire me?" I asked with some apprehension wary of what he might think of my plan.

"It's possible. We're a really good little city and we take care of our young ones. Jason goes to the school. I think I told you its history. It's on the corner of Sixth and Franklin streets. It was built in the spring of 1852 but the heavy snow that winter collapsed the building. They built a two-story frame building to replace it. I can introduce you to Jason's teacher, if you'd like," he said in an off-hand manner.

"I would appreciate it very much, Jake. When would be a good time for you? I could go any day. I have to earn a living and that seems to be the best place to try for a job. Zona said I could work for her but that's not what I want to do. I want to be with children." I looked up at him.

"There's another way, too, Hannah, and that's to be my wife," he said.

"I know, Jake, at least I hope you still want me. Please, just give me some time to be alone and find my way. I do love you but I need to find out just who I am and not in relation to anyone else. Do you understand?" I asked afraid to hear his reply.

"I guess I do, sweetheart, but I don't have to like it." He turned away, then back to me. "I'll be over in the morning with a mount for you. You can keep her at my place where there's a barn but it will your horse. She's young and might take some handling but you can do it." He gave me a peck on the cheek and swung up onto his mare with his usual grace.

I barely slept that night in anticipation of the trip the following day. I looked forward to the ride with Jake both for its destination and for time with him. I knew I loved him but being independent came first, at least for a while.

We rode up to the two-story school and Jake lifted me from the saddle lingering an extra moment with his hands on my waist. He seemed to shake himself and then escorted me into the school. He asked for Stella Smith and the clerk said she'd get her when the morning session ended.

When Miss Smith came into the office, her bright smile landed on Jake and she hurried to him. So again, the green-eyed monster sat on my shoulder. Her medium height brought her just about to my chin and she contained her blonde hair in a mesh snood in the back of her head. Her pristine shirtwaist glowed white before it disappeared into her dark skirt.

"Stella, this is Hannah Jewell and she's looking for a job. I thought you might be able to help," Jake said as he introduced us.

Stella turned to me and held out her hand, not quite as exuberant as when she had entered the room. "I'm glad to meet you, Mrs. Jewell," she said. "Have you had any experience in teaching?"

"I've taught several people to read and I was a librarian back in Philadelphia before the war. I thought I could tutor students or maybe even teach reading. I need to find a job and working with children is where my heart lays, Miss Smith" I said with all of the conviction I could muster.

It seemed a light bulb went on behind her gray eyes. "Are you the one that taught Jason how to read?" she asked. "I was amazed when he first came to school that he was so far advanced for a first grader."

"I suppose you could say I taught him to read obliquely since I taught my niece to read and she in turn taught Jason." I smiled at the thought of that little teacher and her pupil.

"Let's go in and talk to the principal. Do you want to join us Jake?" she asked.

He shook his head and said, "I'll go find Jason and have a bite of his sandwich." He left the office and the light seemed to go out of Miss Smith's eyes. Jake, the rake, seemed to have made another conquest. I fervently hoped the feeling wasn't mutual.

The man sitting in the principal's chair wore spectacles suspended on a chain. He pulled them off as we entered. Miss Smith introduced me and explained my mission to him and he sat back, fingered his watch fob and looked at me with speculation. He also asked about my experience and I repeated what I had told Miss Smith.

"Could you use some help, Stella?" he asked. "You have the largest class in school and there is a little money in our budget for part-time teachers."

"Yes, I could, Mr. O'Brien. Some of the little people need help to read so they can catch up to the rest of the class. I'd be grateful for the help."

I mentally blessed her for her remarks even though jealousy lodged in my breast. "Are you Irish, Mr. O'Brien?" I asked.

"You bet I am, Mrs. Jewell, and proud of it."

"My maiden name is Delaney, so I'm Irish, too, and also proud of it," I said with fervor.

"That clinches it," he said with an expansive smile. "You'll be on probation until we can evaluate your work, but for now you're under Stella's, er, Miss Smith's supervision. Welcome to our staff."

And so began my voyage to find myself and work with children. I now called Miss Smith "Stella" and spent time with the wee ones who needed special help. In between times, I set up the school's library.

Every morning I walked over to Jake's to get my filly, Sophie, and ride her to school. Often after school adjourned for the day, I'd drop by to visit a few minutes with Zona and Lucy. The doctor, often ensconced at his usual table, would stop me to talk with me and his unspoken proposal always shown on his face.

I seldom saw Jake when I went to get my horse or when I returned her. I curried her, fed her and showered love upon her. She was a little hard to handle at first but we became fast friends and she seemed eager to do my bidding.

My meager pay supported me and Andrew's donations of food helped a lot. I had to decide how to prove up on Jade Meadows, but for now, I appreciated my life and my voyage of discovery into who Hannah really was.

Chapter Thirty

As summer neared, I worried what I'd do for employment when school closed for the term. I need not have been concerned since tutoring knew no time limits. A few parents, especially those out my way near Jade Meadows, had heard of me and brought their children to my home for instruction.

Some couldn't pay in hard cash but I took food, sewing, and help on the homestead in payment. I did what I was born to do, I felt, and in that pursuit I found myself and felt comfortable that I was a valuable human being helping others.

Although I seldom saw Jake, I did go over to ride my beautiful Sophie. I often went south of town to visit Andrew and Abby who had grown so much since I first saw her. On one trip out to the Delaney homestead, I had a revealing conversation with my brother.

"Have you any plans for your future, Andrew?" I asked. "I've been waiting for an invitation to your wedding."

"You won't have to wait long, I hope. Phoebe has some decisions to make about her house in town and some other things, too. I want to spruce up the cabin some before we tie the knot. She has furniture she wants to bring out here so I want the surroundings to be worthy." He stopped to catch his breath.

"I think you should caulk the fireplace better, too, so that the smoke goes up the chimney and not into the room," I said and we both laughed. There had been little laughter here when John came to live with us.

"I'll do that, too. What about you and Jake? I don't see him much anymore," Andrew continued.

"I don't see much of him, either. This is the busy time of year for his draying business, I think, and he has to prove up on his homestead. I stable my horse there but he's seldom around," I added.

"You know what I'm really asking, Hannah. When are you two going to get back together? If any two people were ever in love, it was you and Jake."

"I know, Andrew, and it's all my fault. I was so distraught when John came back into my life and then his death made me wonder who I really was. I have been finding out that I'm a valuable person and I needed to know that. Also, I had a lot of guilt about John's death that I had to deal with. In my mind I knew I did all I could to help him but my heart told me if I'd loved him, I'd have done a better job. I don't think his last days were all that pleasant," I said.

"He brought that unpleasantness down on himself. He was an adult and responsible for his own actions in spite of his painful leg," Andrew said vehemently.

"You're right, of course, but it took me a long time to see that. I'm more comfortable with that knowledge now and I love working with children," I explained.

"Don't you think it's time you had children of your own?" my brother asked quietly.

"Nothing would please me more. And maybe after this conversation, I'm ready to move on to the next step in my life. Thanks, Andrew, for being my brother and my sounding board. Now I have to get back to Jade Meadows and my little students." I hugged him and silently thanked the powers that be he was there for me.

Ernie came by the cabin quite often and kept me up to date on the town's happenings. On a late summer morning he brought me some more chickens and I invited him in for a cup of coffee since a chill forecast the coming of autumn.

"So what's the latest with the fire department, Ernie?" I asked. "I haven't heard how the fire hall construction is coming."

"It's almost finished. We had to get an additional loan, this time from Thomas Hartley, to complete the hall. The upstairs is nearly ready and town council meetings will be held on the ground floor. We've already moved the Columbia fire engine into its quarters. We agitated to name the building the Columbia Hall after the engine and, by George, the town fathers agreed." He stopped for breath and gulped some coffee.

"They're already planning a big celebration for its dedication in November, if it's done by that time. All the guys are really excited about it." He finished his coffee and bid me goodbye.

As fall approached, I readied myself for my school duties since I'd been asked to return as a teacher. I enjoyed my work and the friendships I had made at the school. We all cared for children. Andrew's words kept popping into my mind about having children of my own.

Now that I felt comfortable about myself, maybe it was time to think about a family with Jake as its center. His work had slowed with the advent of the territory's weeping fall skies and I saw him more often when I went to get Sophie and when I curried her on my return to the stable. I made the most of these meetings hoping he'd see that I still loved him.

His caution made me realize just how badly I'd hurt him. I couldn't expect him to become passionate again. It would take time.

On a late October day, the sky had lowered and drenched me on my way home from school. I rode Sophie into Jake's barn and wiped her down with a flannel cloth. I dripped water into the straw of her stall but caring for her came first. I put grain in her bin and offered her an apple. She took it daintily with her lips and chewed it with relish.

"You look like a drowned rat, Hannah," I heard Jake say behind me. I turned and looked at his wry smile. Oh, how I had missed that quirky grin on his face.

"You're right, Jake, a drowned rat I am but I'm not made of sugar so I won't melt. I had to tend to Sophie first before myself."

"Come on into the cabin and dry off. I have some coffee on the stove," he said, and I followed him into the warm house. He handed me a towel and poured me a cup of coffee which warmed me both physically and emotionally.

"Thanks, Jake; I guess the cold rain chilled me more than I thought. I haven't seen much of you lately, my friend. I can see the improvements you've made to your homestead. I'm impressed," I rambled on not knowing exactly how to mend the breach between us, but this was a start.

"You might not have seen me but I've kept track of you. You're doing well in your job and with those kids who you tutor at home. Everyone's talking about it." His smoky blue eyes seemed to fill with emotion then he caught himself and smiled. "The town hall celebration dance is set for Nov. 26, Hannah. Will you be my date?"

"Oh, yes, Jake, I'd love to be your date," I said with every fiber of my being.

I fussed over what I'd wear to the dance and decided I'd wear the same gown Zona had given me for that last dance when my life fell apart. I washed my hair, bathed and even used some scent as I got ready for Jake to pick me up in the trap.

Excitement filled me as we drove into town. Rigs were parked everywhere around the new Columbia Hall and the stables were full of horses. The music came out to greet us and Jake swung me down from the trap, held me, kissed me, and held my arm as we went into the hall.

We danced with each other and it seemed every volunteer fireman danced with me, too. Jake took a few turns with Phoebe and Stella, and even Zona who came with Walt, her distinguished boss. I watched as Jake danced with Stella to see if he had any emotion on his face to match the devotion on her countenance. I could detect none.

Soon the crowd started chanting for Zona to do her cakewalk. She held up her hand and said loudly, "I will but you all have to join me in the second chorus." The orchestra began a lively tune and Zona's dance inspired the rest of us as we started kicking and prancing around the floor of the new town hall.

The next dance was a slow one and as Jake and I circled the floor, he asked, "Have you found yourself, yet, Hannah?"

"Yes I have, my dear Jake," I said with no doubt in my mind.

"And who are you, sweetheart?" he asked.

"If you still want me, dearest, I'm your wife." He kissed me passionately as we stood in the middle of the dance floor. The next thing I knew, everyone applauded and congratulated us.

Bibliography

A History of Olympia by Gordon Newell
The Last Wilderness by Murray Morgan
The Writer's Guide to Everyday Life in the 1800's by Marc McCutcheon.
This Was Logging by Ralph W. Andrews
Celebrating the Dream by *The Olympian*
Swift Flows the River by Nard Jones
The Coast reprint of 1909 by Olympia Jaycees
Olympia, Tumwater, and Lacey by Shanna B. Stevenson
The Oyster Was Our World by Cora G. Chase
Olympia's Forgotten Pioneers: The Oblates of Mary Immaculate
     by David Lawrence Nicandri
South Bay—Its History and Its People by South Bay Historical Association.
The History of Tumwater, Volume 3 In A Series—Fortress Tumwater by Don Trosper
Washington State Place Names by James W. Phillips
Washington State Historical Society

Contributors:

Edwin Blake
Rick Gibbons
Carolyn Dibble
Paul Moody
Marge Hitchcock

Proof readers:

Irene Dornan
Barbara Morris
Lois Wilson
Esther Rust
Carolyn Dibble
Billie Wayt

978-0-595-68201-0
0-595-68201-4

Printed in the United States
75289LV00004B/7-162